# PERFECT MURDER

David Conrad

iUniverse, Inc.
New York   Bloomington

iUniverse books may be ordered through booksellers or by contacting:

iUniverse
1663 Liberty Drive
Bloomington, IN 47403
www.iuniverse.com
1-800-Authors (1-800-288-4677)

Because of the dynamic nature of the Internet, any Web addresses or links contained in this book may have changed since publication and may no longer be valid. The views expressed in this work are solely those of the author and do not necessarily reflect the views of the publisher, and the publisher hereby disclaims any responsibility for them.

ISBN: 978-1-4401-6556-6 (sc)
ISBN: 978-1-4401-6555-9 (hc)
ISBN: 978-1-4401-6557-3 (ebook)

Printed in the United States of America

iUniverse rev. date: 11/09/2009

# CHAPTER 1

Sheriff Marcus Dixon nosed his 1935 Chevrolet coupe into the parking space on the Circle in Zeigler, Illinois. He swung his long legs out of the car, closed the door, and looked up apprehensively at the lone brick building that dominated the Circle. He would rather have been doing almost anything else. Missing persons investigations were usually a head-ache and this one could turn out to be a real pain in the ass. The person who was missing was the wife of Richard Newcombe, the manager of the Consolidation Coal Company mine in Zeigler and about the most unpopular man in the county.

Marcus took his time walking through the grassy circular park that was, in effect, the town square. He stopped to speak with three older men in worn overalls who sat on a bench. One of them had a bad cough and talked in a whisper. *Black lung*, Marcus thought. Probably the reason all three of them were sitting there instead of working in the mine today. Marcus had lived in the coal belt all of his life, but still he could not get used to the harsh reality of coalminers' lives. On the other hand, he told himself, these three men were lucky to be sitting there in the sun on a nice day. It was a lot safer than working down in the mine. As he walked past a granite monument with a bronze plaque memorializing thirteen miners killed in the 1923 explosion in Number 3 Mine, Marcus nodded his head. *Yes, it was safer here in the park than down in the mine.*

Zeigler was a coal town, pure and simple. The office of Consolidation Coal, which sat in the center of the Circle, was the closest thing Zeigler had to a city hall.  Around the outside of the Circle were uniform brick buildings, including the company store, a haberdashery, three saloons, a café, and a drug store, many of them owned by Consolidation Coal, as were most of the houses in town.

Marcus walked up the steps to the building and entered the office of the manager. Maureen Zalesky sat typing a letter to the home office in Chicago. She looked up to see the sheriff come through the double doors.

"Well, good morning, Marcus," she smiled sweetly "What are you doing here in Zeigler?"

"Here to see Mr. Newcombe, Maureen. How have you been? How's old Alfred?"

"He's OK, I guess. Number 3 is shut down today, so he's probably down at Hunker's drinking beer. How have you been? You married yet?"

"Nope. Not since all the girls like you are taken, Maureen."

"Well, you had your chance, Marcus."

"I remember. What about Mr. Newcombe?"

"He's in. I'll buzz him."

She pressed a button and spoke into a box. "Sheriff Dixon is here to see you, Mr. Newcombe."

"All right, send him in," the box answered.

Richard Newcombe sat at a large mahogany desk. He was a handsome fellow, about thirty-five. He wore a dark suit, white shirt and silk tie. Marcus, in his khaki shirt and pants, would have bet that Newcombe was the only man in Zeigler wearing a suit that day.  He did not rise to greet Marcus.

"I suppose you're here about Amanda. I told everything I know to Chief Callum. I figured he would be handling things."

"He asked for my help. And we may call in the state people, depending on how things develop."

"Have a seat. I'll help you if I can."

Marcus eased into a wooden captain's chair and pulled a small notebook from the pocket of his shirt.

"Your wife, Amanda, is missing—has been since day before yesterday. Right?"

"Yeah. That's right. She was not there when I came home from the office that evening."

"Did you go home for lunch?"

"No. It was the housekeeper's day off."

"Did she leave a note or any indication of where she had gone?"

"Nothing. But her suitcase and some of her clothes are missing. Most of her make-up and that sort of stuff is gone too."

"Do you have any idea where she is? Has she ever just left before?"

"I have no idea. She's never done anything like this before."

"How long have you been married?"

"Three years—no children."

"And where is her home town?"

"She grew up in Chicago. She has a few relatives there—her mother and father and a sister and a few others."

"How's your marriage? Any problems?"

Newcombe looked at Marcus sharply. "That's pretty personal, isn't it?"

"As personal as it gets, but that's the sort of thing we have to look into. What's the answer?"

Newcombe stood and walked to the window. He looked out over Zeigler, the town that he practically ran.

"We had our ups and downs. Amanda was a city girl. She never really adjusted to Southern Illinois—too many rednecks I guess."

"I notice you are referring to her in the past tense."

"Oh, yeah. I guess I was just thinking about her being gone."

"Have her parents been notified that she is missing?"

"I called them yesterday. Her father is coming down here by car today."

"Is there anything you can tell me that will help us find your wife?"

"I've wracked my brain. I can't come up with a thing. Do you think you can find her?"

"Well, so far we don't have much to work with. It would help if you would give permission to go through her things at your home. I might find something to get us started."

"Sure. Go ahead. I'll phone the housekeeper and tell her you are coming."

"That would be good. We're going to do everything we can to find your wife, Mr. Newcombe. If you think of something, give my office a call."

As Marcus walked through the outer office, Maureen rose from her desk and walked with him to the doors.

"You should come over to Zeigler more often, Marcus," she said softly. "You used to come all the time."

Marcus smiled. "Well, I had a good reason to come in those days, didn't I?"

"It was fun, wasn't it?"

"It was that. But you're married now, and I have a big county to cover. But I'll be seeing you from time to time, Maureen."

"Make sure you do that." Maureen put her hand gently on his arm.

Marcus had always liked Maureen. Her dark red hair, green eyes, and abundant curves made it hard not to like her. Back when they were going together, they *did* have good times, but now her obvious come-on was making Marcus uncomfortable. She was married, and although they had parted on good terms, he was not interested in a little extra marital activity with her. But then maybe she was just teasing him for the fun of it. That was Maureen—she was a great tease. As he walked awkwardly back to his car, Marcus smiled to himself. One thing was certain—if Maureen had wanted to get a rise out of him, it had certainly worked.

As Marcus drove the few blocks to the mine manager's house, he thought about Zeigler, the second largest town in his county. It was not an ugly town, as coal towns go. Most of the houses had been built by the company. There were few variations, but it was better construction than the shanties and shotgun houses of other towns in the coal belt. The houses lined up in neat rows along paved streets, giving the impression of financial stability. But Marcus knew that the families living in the company houses were barely above the poverty line. The Depression was nothing new to them. They had always been poor.

Newcombe's house was the largest in Zeigler. Built in the Queen Anne style, it sat on a hill across town from the entry to the mine.

Marcus parked in front, walked on the sidewalk through a well kept lawn and up the steps of the front porch. He rapped politely with the brass knocker, and the door opened quickly revealing a middle-aged woman wearing an apron.

"Hello Sheriff," the woman said with a Polish accent. "My name is Freddie Albagetti. Mr. Newcombe said you was coming."

"Nice to meet you—uh, Freddie. How about we sit down and talk for a while before I look around."

"Sure, Sheriff. I'll make some coffee. Let's go in the kitchen."

"My favorite place. So what does "Freddie" stand for—Frederica?"

"Yeah, Frederica. I guess the other choice was Fred, but don't call me that," she added with a wry smile.

"OK, I won't—Freddie."

As she made coffee, Marcus watched carefully. It was obviously Freddie's kitchen. Everything was neat and in place. When she wanted something—a match to light the gas stove or a coffee container—she reached without thinking to the right place. She seemed perfectly at ease.

"How long have you worked here, Freddie?"

"Four years. I worked for Mr. Brewer, the other manager. I started here after my husband died in the mine—roof-fall."

"Any children?"

"Two. They're both grown. "

"What kind of woman is Mrs. Newcombe?"

"Miss Amanda? Well, she's a quiet one. Stays in her room a lot. She don't make friends easy. She don't even go to church. Mostly she just reads books and writes letters."

"What does she look like? I noticed there was no picture of her on Mr. Newcombe's desk."

"She don't like to have her picture made. She don't even like mirrors in the house."

"Is she pretty?"

"You know, I would say she's kinda pretty. She's got brunette hair, nice complexion, and a good figure. She could look a lot better if she paid more attention to fixin' herself up."

"How does she get along with Newcombe?"

"Well, I guess I shouldn't say it, but they ain't the most loving couple. They eat their meals without talking much, and lots of evenings he just sits and plays the radio. In the summer he's out on the porch listening to the Cardinal games and smoking cigarettes. Some evenings he goes out."

"Goes out? Where does he go?"

"I don't know. He just gets in that nice car of his and leaves. Doesn't say anything. He just goes."

Marcus had finished his coffee.

"Freddie, let's go look around Mrs. Newcombe's bedroom."

The bedroom was upstairs in the front of the house. Freddie led Marcus to it and pointed to a bedroom across the hall.

"That's where Mister Newcombe sleeps."

Amanda's bedroom was surprisingly Spartan. A nice bed, a few chairs and a chest of drawers, but nothing frilly and very few decorations. The only pictures were photographs of a middle-aged couple, probably her parents.

Marcus worked around the room opening drawers, looking in the closet, and checking the storage boxes on shelves.

The most prominent feature of the room was books—several hundred of them. They lined shelves and filled two large book cases. Stacks of magazines stood in one corner. Marcus checked some of the titles—mostly romance novels, but a liberal smattering of murder mysteries and crime magazines.

When he finished, Marcus turned to Freddie and asked, "What's missing?"

"As far as I can tell, it's some of her clothes, a few pairs of shoes, and some of her make-up and a hairbrush—stuff like that. And one other thing—a pillow off the bed."

"Suitcase?"

"Yes, that too."

Marcus sat at the writing desk and looked into all the drawers. One of them was locked.

"You have a key for this?" he asked.

"No. She always keeps that draw locked. I think she has the key on a little chain around her neck."

"I'm going to have to open it," Marcus said.

"They won't like that."

"Can't be helped."

Marcus opened his pocket knife and worked the bolt of the lock out of its slot. Inside, he found bundles of letters, most of them with Chicago postmarks. Some were from people named Littleton, mostly women's first names. Marcus opened a few of these—they appeared to be from Amanda's mother and sister. Several bundles were postmarked Chicago, but there were no return addresses. Marcus tried to read three or four of them and found they were written in some sort of code. He showed the letters to Freddie.

"You know anything about this?"

"Well, she was always reading and writing letters. Did it for an hour or two every day. And she was awfully particular about the mail. When it came, I was to bring her mail directly to her bedroom. She was always sitting there waiting for it."

"Now I want to see Newcombe's room across the hall."

The bedroom was quite a contrast. Newcombe had sports and family pictures on the walls, but there were no books. His drawers were filled with expensive clothing. The closet held at least a dozen good suits and half a dozen sports coats. On a high shelf there were four hat boxes. The floor of the closet was lined with well-made shoes, including two pairs of two-toned wing-tips, one brown and white and one black and white.

"He's quite a dresser, isn't he?" Marcus commented.

"Oh yes. He spends more time on his appearance than she does."

"Where's the bathroom."

"You want to use it?"

"No, Freddie," Marcus smiled. "I want to examine it."

Again, there was nothing feminine about the bathroom. It could have been the bathroom in any decent hotel. The medicine cabinet revealed nothing interesting. The medications were nothing more than aspirin and sleeping pills. The Newcombes must be healthy, Marcus thought.

Next, he turned to Freddie and asked, "Does this house have a basement?"

"Yes. I'll show you."

It was a full basement with a huge coal furnace in the center. Since the weather was warm, there was no fire in the furnace. Marcus opened the door and lit a match to see inside—nothing but clinkers.

*At least there are no charred human remains*, Marcus told himself with some relief. Next, he checked the dimly lit coal room and found the coal to be only a foot or so deep, not enough to cover a body. Then he carefully examined the concrete floor and walls of the basement and looked in two storage rooms. No signs of fresh concrete work.

"Now, Freddie, I want to examine the attic."

"Nothing up there, Sheriff. Nothing at all."

"Let's look anyhow."

Freddie was right. There was nothing in the attic but dust.

"I'm done now, except for looking over the grounds."

"You don't need me for that. It's a big yard. They have a gardener. He comes two days a week. Name's Henry Stanhouse. Old fellow. Can't work in the mine no more because of the black lung. He keeps the grass mowed and the bushes trimmed."

"Do you know where he lives?"

"I'm not sure. They can tell you down at Hunker's. He hangs out there a lot."

"Freddie. You have been a big help. If you think of anything else, give me a call.

"I will, Sheriff. I hope you find her. I hope she's all right."

Marcus spent twenty minutes looking around the extensive grounds. He could not find any recently disturbed ground, except maybe the flower beds. They were well kept but did not seem to be freshly worked. He noted that there were no nearby neighbors and that the garage in back of the house and the driveway that came up from a side street were well screened by trees and shrubbery.

Hunker's Place was a typical coal town bar. It was so dark inside that Marcus had to stop and wait for his eyes to adjust after he entered. Miners like it dark. As he waited, he took in the odor of the place—stale air permeated with the smell of the sawdust on the floor, cigarette smoke, beer, and male perspiration. There were other places like Hunker's in Zeigler, one for the Poles, Lithuanians, and Bohemians and one for the Italians. Hunker's catered to the types who had migrated to Southern Illinois from West Virginia and Kentucky. Marcus could hear the Appalachian accents as two patrons argued amiably but loudly over who was the best fighter, Joe Louis or Gene Tunney. To call any of these men rednecks might start a fight, but they would never answer to any fancy anthropologist's classifications such as Anglo-Americans. They considered themselves true Americans, a status they were not ready to afford the Bohunks and the Italians.

Coal miners liked to relax in places like Hunker's. Mining was mind-numbing, back-breaking, dangerous work. After work or when they were laid off, they gathered in their bars, ate the spicy meats and sandwiches at the free lunch counter, and talked with their friends. Wives and children were not welcome. The only women there were likely to be of fairly easy virtue, probably for a price. One of the saloons in town was run by the widow of a miner killed in the fire of 1923.

Marcus asked the bartender if Henry Stanhouse was there, and he pointed to a grey-haired fellow sitting in the corner. As Marcus made his way through the tables, he passed Alfred Zalesky sitting with three other men.

"Well, look who's here. It's the High Sheriff. How you doin' Marcus?" Zalesky was obviously a little drunk. His tone was irritating, but Marcus expected it. Zalesky was always irritating and usually a little drunk.

"Here on a little business, Alfred. How you doin'?"

"Fine as frog hair split four ways."

The three men laughed.

"Maureen talks about you a lot, Marcus."

"Yeah, we used to run around together."

"I know." Alfred took a good pull on his beer. "Well, don't work too hard."

"Sure. Don't work too hard yourself."

"You sure as hell don't have to worry about me doin' that."

The three men laughed again.

Marcus walked on, wishing he had come up with a good rejoinder. Zalesky was being a smart ass and the three laughers were his audience.

But Marcus had other fish to fry. He approached Henry Stanhouse's table.

"Mind if I join you? I'm Sheriff Dixon."

"I see the badge. Go ahead and set. What do you want?"

Stanhouse spoke with the hoarse voice that comes with black lung. He was painfully thin, and his pallor belied the fact that he worked outdoors.

"You're the gardener at the Newcombe place, aren't you?"

"That's right."

"Did you work there two days ago?"

"Yep. Worked all day."

"Did you ever see Mrs. Newcombe while you were there?"

"No."

"Did you see anyone come and go during the day?"

"Some. Newcombe—he went to work about 8:30, like usual. A couple of people made deliveries around back. I couldn't tell much about them from where I was. Why are you asking?"

"Investigation. Mrs. Newcombe is missing. When did Newcombe come home from work?"

"Don't know. I quit about four. I was plumb wore out."

"When was the last time you saw Mrs. Newcombe?"

"Hardly ever see her. Maybe once last week. She never comes out in the yard."

"All right, Alfred. Thanks for your help."

As Marcus drove back to Franklin, he sorted through what he had learned. The Newcombes were obviously not a happy couple. Amanda showed every sign of being lonely and dissatisfied. Her letters interested him, especially the ones written in code. What was that all about? The missing clothes and other personal things might indicate that she simply got fed up with her life, packed a few things and left. But no one saw her leave. Newcombe's car still sat in the garage, so she couldn't have taken it. So how could she leave without a car and go very far and completely disappear?

Newcombe had to be a suspect. Husbands usually are until proven otherwise. He had certainly not seemed terribly distraught. In fact, he was already thinking of her in the past tense. Maybe he had something to do with her absence. They did seem like an odd match. A barely pretty, reclusive wife married to a fellow with the good looks and manners of a successful executive.

And where did Maureen Zalesky fit into the picture? It was a cinch that she was not Newcombe's secretary solely because of her secretarial skills. Maureen was no dummy, but at best she had one course in typing in high school. Shorthand was out of the question. No, Maureen was there because of her good looks and maybe more. Marcus did not figure Maureen was the kind of girl who would say no to a fellow like Newcombe, especially since he was her boss.

What if Newcombe, who obviously thought he was awfully superior and clever, had decided to get rid of his unhappy wife by killing her and making it look like she had just run off and disappeared. That would free him to play around with ladies like Maureen and maybe others. About the only thing he seemed to know for sure about Amanda's absence was that some of her things were missing, the sort of things a woman would take on a trip. Maybe that was part of the plan. Maybe Newcombe had disposed of those things in the same place he had hidden Amanda's body. For the whole thing to work, that would have to be some place where the body and the other things would never be found. Were there such places? Marcus knew there were—lots of them in his and surrounding counties.

So, did Richard Newcombe think he was smart enough to commit a perfect murder? Sometimes, a wife just up and leaves her husband. It's usually the other way around, but every now and then it's the wife that leaves. Was that what Newcombe wanted everyone to believe?

One thing was sure—there was a whole lot more investigating to be done. People don't just disappear. Amanda Newcombe had to be somewhere.

# CHAPTER 2

Franklin, Illinois was a larger town than Zeigler and more than just a coal town. For one thing, it was the county seat. The Jefferson County court house sat in the middle of the town square. Only two years old, the hulking stone building had replaced an antiquated and hopeless edifice built in the 1870's. The new court house was a product of the Works Progress Administration, and, to say the least, the architectural style, best described as Depression Art Deco, was something of a shock to the citizenry. They had not been consulted about it, and the local Republicans resented it greatly, saying it was another one of Roosevelt's boondoggles. But there were so few Republicans in the county that nobody paid much attention to their grumblings. In point of fact, the new court house was a fine, stoutly constructed building that would be there for generations to come. As for architectural style, if the other downtown buildings and all the fine homes on Mulberry Street were an indication, there was not much architectural taste in Franklin anyhow.

Because it was well past lunch time, Marcus parked in the sheriff's parking space behind the Court House and walked across the street to the City Café. The café had once been a clothing store, but the depression had ended its 50-year tenure. To call the present establishment a café was stretching a point since it really was little more than a diner. No more than twenty feet wide, it accommodated only a few tables. Most of the customers sat on stools at the long counter that ran half the length of the building. The café served only breakfast and lunch, and it was usually busy. As Marcus entered, he heard the familiar clatter of dishes and a sizzling sound that came from the long grill sitting against the side wall.

Marcus eased onto a stool and spoke to several of his neighbors, including the sole proprietor and main attraction of the City Café, Mary Ellen Selvedge. In fact, Mary Ellen was the reason Marcus frequented the place, aside from her acceptable food. Marcus, like the other male patrons, found it a pleasure just to watch Mary Ellen as she moved efficiently up and down the counter, serving plates of food, filling coffee cups, flipping burger patties on the grill, turning piles of onions cooking in bacon grease, cracking eggs with one hand as she poured pancake batter with the other, and all the while carrying on a lively conversation with just about everyone in the place, all of whom she seemed to know well.

No doubt about it, Mary Ellen was a fine looking young woman. Neither the white apron tied around her trim waist nor the starched cotton blouse that never seemed to get a spot of grease on it, could conceal her perfect figure. And with her strawberry-blond hair swept up in the back, it was even stimulating just to look at the back of her neck as she worked at the grill. She was always on the move, but she never seemed in a hurry or flustered.

Mary Ellen set a steaming cup of coffee in front of Marcus and smiled in a special way that others noticed and envied.

"Afternoon, Marcus. You hungry?"

"Mary Ellen, I'm always hungry."

"You want the usual?"

"How'd you guess?"

She opened the refrigerator and took out an eight ounce beef steak. With an easy motion, she laid the steak on the grill and covered it with an iron bar with a wooden handle attached that had been heating on the grill. Then she tossed a handful of shredded potatoes on the grill and poured a small amount of oil on it from a metal pitcher.

Mary Ellen had other customers waiting for their orders, but she turned to Marcus and poured more coffee for him.

"What's new in the sheriff business?" she asked.

Marcus was tempted to tell her about the missing Amanda Newcombe, but that would have been the equivalent of releasing the story to the press since the City Café was the news center of Franklin and Mary Ellen was the purveyor. Marcus wasn't ready to go public.

"Nothing I can talk about."

"Sounds interesting."

"You'll find out soon enough. How's my steak coming?"

"Changing the subject, eh?"

"Yeah, I guess so."

A customer down the counter called out, "Hey Mary Ellen quit flirting with the Sheriff and get me my burger."

"OK, Harry. Just wait while I put some salt peter on it."

This brought a good laugh from the customers up and down the line.

Marcus finished his steak and paid his check. As he left the café, one of the patrons said to another, "You ever seen what they call slow motion in the movies? Well, that's what the sheriff reminds me of."

The other nodded, "Yeah, but he sure as hell wasn't slow when he played end for the high school football team. Faster than greased lightning—great hands. He was one of the best we ever had. He played end for the Illini when he went to college up there at Champaign. In fact, he was All American. Played in one of them All Star games in Chicago—you know, the best college boys against the best pro team. I think it was the Green Bay Packers that year."

"He looks like he could suit up right now."

"Yeah. He stays in good shape, and he moves fast when he has to."

The Sheriff's Office was on the first floor of the Court House. The county jail was on the third floor, along with a small apartment that was one of the benefits of being sheriff. The pay was not great, but at least the sheriff had a place to live without cost. Often, the sheriff's wife did the cooking for the prisoners in jail and the jailors, but since Marcus was not married, there was a hired cook, a Mrs. Fallon.

Marcus walked into his office and stopped to check with the desk sergeant, Orville Bailey. "What's happening, Orv?" he asked.

"No much, Sheriff. Got a complaint about some missing cattle down at Bumcombe, and there was a fight at Dempsey's Bar. Hank and Wilford went over there and settled things down."

"Did they arrest anyone?"

"Nope. It was a fair fight. Nobody got hurt much."

Marcus nodded and walked back to his own office. He was looking over some state police bulletins when he glanced out the window to see a large Packard parking in the visitor's parking space. A uniformed chauffeur got out of the car and opened the door for a well-dressed man wearing a Homburg hat. The man looked up at the Court House, said something to the driver, and walked toward the entry.

*I'll bet this is the missing woman's father,* Marcus told himself. Shortly, he heard the man saying he wanted to see the sheriff.

Marcus stood to shake hands. "I'm Sheriff Dixon. How can I help you?"

The man settled into a chair without being asked and eyed Marcus skeptically. "Sheriff, I am Randolph Littleton. I am president of the Consolidation Coal Company, and my daughter is the wife of Richard Newcombe. She is missing. I want to know what you are doing about it."

"We're investigating," Marcus said evenly.

"Well, I asked the same question of the police chief in Zeigler—I believe his name is Callum (Marcus nodded)—and he had no answer. It's obvious to me that he has no idea what he's doing."

"He has asked for my help, and we will call in the state police if they are needed."

"State police? You mean the Highway Patrol?"

"They have a criminal investigation division, but we haven't determined that there has been a crime. At this point, it is a missing person case."

"Why don't you call in the FBI?"

"I will if it this turns out to be a kidnapping."

"So you are leading the investigation?"

"Yes."

"And what is the size of your staff?"

"Well, there are seven of us—me, a sergeant, and five deputies."

"No detectives?"

"Just me."

"How long have you been sheriff, and what is your training as a detective?"

"Look Mr. Littleton, I'm the one who should be asking the questions. You seem to have doubts about our abilities down here in Southern Illinois to conduct a police investigation. I know we are not like your big police force in Chicago, but we probably have a better record for honesty, and we know what we are doing."

Littleton relaxed slightly. "You have a point, Sheriff. It's just that I'm concerned about my daughter."

"I can understand that."

"One more thing, Sheriff, and I hope you will take this in the way it is intended. My company has its own police force, including some well trained detectives. I can offer them to help you."

"I would be happy to have their help, Mr. Littleton, but I hope you will take this the way it is intended—you could find very few people who would be less welcome in this county than your company police. Nobody around here would be willing to cooperate with them."

"Why is that?"

"Company police—the bulls—they have cracked the heads of too many strikers to be very popular around here. But the investigation may lead to Chicago since that is where Amanda Newcombe is from. Maybe up there . . . ."

"Consider it done. They will be at your disposal. The chief is named Kelly. His office is in Chicago. I'll have him contact you."

Marcus gave Littleton a brief outline of what his investigation had revealed that morning. Littleton listened carefully but made no comment. When Marcus was done, he leaned forward and asked, "So, what have you concluded?"

"It's too early for conclusions."

Littleton seemed dissatisfied but changed the subject. "You mentioned that you had questions for me," he said.

"Yes. Tell me about your daughter. What's she like?"

"Amanda is 27 years old. She grew up on the north side of Chicago. We have a home there. She attended private schools and Northwestern University. She married Newcombe three years ago. He was a management trainee in the main office of Consolidation Coal at the time."

"What's she like as a person?"

"My wife could answer that question better than I. Most of my time is spent running Consolidation Coal. About all I can say is that around me Mary Ellen is quiet and reserved. She never wanted to be a debutante, although she could have been and her mother wanted it badly. She seems to be some sort of intellectual—reads poetry and novels and likes to go to plays and movies. I suppose she was bored living in Zeigler. It's such a small town."

"Not many plays and poetry readings in Zeigler," Marcus commented.

"I'm not even sure Amanda is very close to her mother or her sister. As I said, she is pretty reserved."

"What about boyfriends before she was married? Were there any?"

"One. His name was Hanley Friedman. She met him at Northwestern. He fancied himself a poet or novelist or something like that. Never had a job. He may have even been Jewish . . . completely unacceptable. My wife and I discouraged that relationship."

"And where did she meet Newcombe?"

"He met her at a company party and asked my permission to see her."

"What happened to Hanley Friedman?"

"That, I don't know."

"Let me ask this, Mr. Littleton. Do you have any ideas about where your daughter may be or what might have happened to her?"

"Sheriff, I thought about it a lot on the way down here. I don't know enough about the situation to come up with a theory. Do you have one?

"Obviously, there are two basic possibilities: either she has left of her own accord—and there is some evidence of that—or she has been abducted, for which there is no evidence except the fact that she is missing."

"All right, Sheriff, I'll leave you to your work now. I'll return to Chicago tomorrow. Here's my card. Please let me know when you have any solid information."

"Mr. Littleton, I am going to do everything I can to find your daughter."

"Thank you Sheriff. I'm counting on you doing just that."

When Littleton left, Sergeant Bailey stuck his head in the door and said, "Harold Anderson is waiting to see you."

Marcus muttered, "Uh oh. I guess the word is out. OK, tell him to come in."

Anderson was the editor of the *Jefferson County Enterprise,* the leading newspaper in the county. He pointed back out the door and said, "That was Randolph Littleton, wasn't it?"

Marcus nodded.

"Then it must be true. His daughter has been kidnapped or murdered or something like that. This is a big story."

"Cool down, Harold. So far I can't tell you anything."

"Cool down! This may be the biggest thing that has happened around here. The *Enterprise* is just a country weekly. We don't get a big story very often.

"What makes you think it's a big story?"

"Good God, don't you realize who this woman is? She's a coal heiress. Randolph Littleton is the head of the Consolidation Coal Company. This will be all over the Chicago papers when it gets out."

"As I said, I can't tell you anything."

"Well, when can you tell me something?"

"Don't know, Harold. I'll let you know when I have some solid information."

Anderson was not satisfied. "At least give me something. Can I print that she is missing?"

"OK."

"And that you are investigating?"

"Yeah, and that's about it."

"Marcus, I'm counting on you to give me a call."

"I will, but I need to get to work now."

Anderson left muttering to himself about freedom of the press, and Marcus sighed in relief. He called Sergeant Bailey into his office and said, "Orville, check through all that pile of paperwork we get and see if you have anything on a Hanley Friedman, and call the state crime center and ask them about him. I'm going to drive over to DuQuoin and talk to someone at the Illinois Central Depot."

There was no railroad passenger service in Jefferson County—plenty of coal trains but no passenger. The nearest place to catch a train was DuQuoin, twenty miles west. DuQuoin was on the main line of the Illinois Central Railroad which ran from Chicago to New Orleans.

Marcus knew the depot in DuQuoin well. He had used it often when he went off to Champaign and the University of Illinois. In fact, he had a vague memory of the train schedules and even knew the names of two trains—*The City of New Orleans* and *the Illini*. If he thought hard enough, he could probably remember the name of one of the fancy dining cars with its linen table cloths, china, and white-coated waiters.

Marcus parked in the row of spaces next to the station. Like many others on the Illinois Central, the station was an oblong two story brick building lying parallel to the tracks. It had the waiting room in one end and the baggage room in the other. Between them was the ticket office and the three sided portico peculiar to most train stations that allowed the telegrapher and ticket agent, usually the same person, to look both ways down the tracks.

As Marcus walked into the waiting room he was greeted by the like-no-other odor of a train station, a mix of stale tobacco smoke, pine oil disinfectant, and poorly kept rest rooms. Marcus could hear the click- clack of the telegraph behind the ticket agent's window. He stepped up to the ticket window and waited while the agent finished at the telegraph key. When he finally came to the window, Marcus said, "Howdy. I'm Sheriff Dixon from Jefferson County. I'm investigation the disappearance of a young woman from Zeigler, and I would like to ask you a few questions."

The ticket agent looked to be in his early sixties—not far from a highly prized railroad retirement. He wore a black bow tie and a white shirt with brass buttons on the collar engraved with the letters IC. His flat-topped black cap with a brass IC emblem sat on the desk behind him, ready to go on his head when he went out on the platform.

"Sure thing, Sheriff. My name's Howard Fraley. What do you want to know?"

"Were you on duty day before yesterday?"

"Yep. I'm the day man. I'm on duty most days."

"Then there's a night man?"

"That's right. I reckon he's home sleeping. In fact there's three of us. We have 22 trains a day coming through here. Keeps us busy."

"I'm interested in passenger trains during the day."

"Goin' which way?"

"Both ways."

"Well we have eight altogether. There's the 8:14 northbound and . . ."

"That's OK. I don't need all the times. Do you remember a young woman, well dressed, kind of pretty, buying a ticket the day before yesterday?"

"You mean by herself?"

"Yes, or with someone."

"That's two different things. I don't remember any single young women buying a ticket that day, and I think I would remember if one did. But we sell a lot of tickets to young couples. Probably sold several that day."

"Do you remember any of them well enough to describe them?"

"Naw. Not really. You say she is kind of pretty?"

"Yes. Nothing fancy, but sort of pretty. She was probably wearing big city type clothes."

"Well, I'll tell you Sheriff—don't let this white hair fool you. I notice pretty women—always have. What color hair does she have?"

"I'm not sure. We don't have a picture of her yet."

"There was one couple that might fit. They bought one-way tickets to Carbondale."

"Had you ever seen them before?"

"No. But she was kind of pretty, like you said."

"What did he look like?"

"Nothing special. He had long hair; that's all I remember."

"Mr. Fraley, I want to thank you for your help."

"You bet, Sheriff. I hope you find her."

As he drove back to Franklin, Marcus thought about how things were going. He had told Randolph Littleton that he and his department knew what they were doing, but he had to admit to himself that he was not as confident as that sounded. Sure, he had investigated missing person cases before, even a few murders and one kidnapping. But he had only been a sheriff for two years, and this case was different. If it turned out to be a murder or kidnapping of a coal heiress, there would be a lot of publicity and pressure—he had already felt some of it. Was he ready for something like that?

Marcus had never been troubled with self doubt. Often, when he was playing football, his teammates got anxious and stressed out before a big game, but he was usually the one that remained calm. Fear of failure was something that did not keep him awake at night. Marcus knew that he was not a stereotypical dumb football player. He had done well at the university, especially in the liberal arts, although he had majored in physical education. He figured he had the intelligence to be a good detective, but he was also smart enough to realize that to be one he needed more experience and professional training.

Then there was the matter of the people under Marcus—his six man force. They were all good men, able to do their jobs as deputies in a county like Jefferson. But none of them had ever had any real police training. None of them had ever been to college, and most of them had never been very far out of Southern Illinois. Randolph Littleton had probably been justified in questioning his force's readiness to handle an important case.

By the time Marcus had thought through all of this, he was driving into the outskirts of Franklin. It was time to face the actual situation, which was really quite simple. He was the Sheriff of Jefferson County, this was his case to handle, and he would just have to work with what he had.

One thing was sure—he sure as hell needed a picture and a better description of Amanda Newcombe. It had been dumb of him to start his investigation without that.

# CHAPTER 3

It was nearly dark when Marcus got back to the Court House. He dropped by his office to see if there were any messages. Sergeant Bailey had gone home for the day and Deputy Hank Cronnin was sitting at his desk.

"Anything new?" Marcus asked.

"Nothing," Cronnin answered. "I'm just sitting here in case there's a call. I don't think I'll go on patrol tonight."

"All right. I'm going upstairs and relax."

Marcus took the elevator to the third floor. There were very few elevators in Franklin —no tall buildings. Even this one was not for public use. It went to the court rooms and judges' offices on the second floor and jail and sheriff's apartment on the third floor. For security reasons, it required a key.

Marcus got off on the third floor and walked past the jail, pausing for a moment to speak to the jailer. In his apartment he went first to the refrigerator and took out a Budweiser. He had the same thought he always had when he took the first drink:

*Five years ago it was illegal as all hell to drink this stuff. I would have to arrest myself for consuming alcohol.* He opened a can of pink salmon, poured the contents on a plate, and began eating with a fork, accompanying it with a dozen saltine crackers. *Not bad,* he told himself. *A bachelor can't afford to waste his time cooking fancy meals.*

With the brown beer bottle in his hand, Marcus walked to one of his two windows and looked out over the west side of Franklin. He watched the glowing red ball of the sun sink below the flat horizon. A few electric lights were already showing in the windows of the houses, and others came on as he watched. Franklin wasn't a bad town—not a great one but not a bad one. The people there were doing their best to recover what they had lost in the Depression. Many of them were still without jobs, but they were getting by. They planted gardens in their back yards, they wore ten-year old clothing, and they put cardboard in their shoes where there were holes in the soles. Unemployed men spent much of their time hunting and fishing, telling themselves they were putting meat on the table.

Marcus took a drink from the Budweiser. At least he had a job— sheriff of Jefferson County. He often marveled at how that happened. When he graduated from the university there were no jobs for physical education majors, not even one who was a big star in football. He had planned to become a coach, maybe eventually at some college, but there were no jobs, not even at a small high school. When old Sheriff Billings died of a heart attack, Marcus ran in the next primary election to replace him simply because he needed a job. Several others ran also, one or two with more experience, but Marcus won easily. He assumed it was because of his football fame and not because he was well qualified to be sheriff. There certainly were times when he asked himself if he knew what he was doing as a sheriff. But that was true of many sheriffs when they began. There were no schools to train sheriffs—they had to learn on the job.

Most people in the county didn't seem to care if the sheriff was not a real professional. They knew the county needed a sheriff to enforce the laws, but the less they saw of him, the better. Many in the county would be happy if the sheriff and his deputies all stayed in the far end of the county—until there was a murder or someone got robbed. Other disputes could be settled in the usual ways, sometimes with fights, often by simply waiting things out. In his two years as sheriff, Marcus had investigated several murders, but they were simple affairs—a fight that got out of hand, a husband that caught his wife in bed with another man. He had arrested two suspects for murder. Both were easily convicted and sent to Joliet for life. One other murder suspect had fled the state right after the crime. He was rumored to be in California, but there was no way to go after him.

Marcus felt pretty good about his first two years as sheriff. He had learned a lot, but he was concerned about the Newcombe case. This was different. No real clues, no way to know at this point where Amanda Newcombe was or what had happened to her. Did he have the skills to handle a case like this? For that matter, what kind of case was it? A kidnapping? An abduction and murder? A runaway wife?

One thing was clear. The monkey was on his back. There was no other legal authority to take charge of this case. Sure, Chief Callum in Zeigler had jurisdiction, but he had handed the case to Marcus right away. He did not want to deal with Richard Newcombe.

Marcus stood at the window looking out over the now dark town. Above it, Venus, the Evening Star, shone with startling brilliance in the still blue sky. The beer bottle in Marcus's hand was no longer cold, so he walked to the kitchen sink and poured out the remaining contents. Just then, the direct line phone from his office rang. Marcus answered it, and Deputy Cronnin said, "You have a *personal* call, Sheriff."

Marcus was puzzled by the cloying tone in Cronnin's voice. He told him to transfer the call and heard, "Marcus, this is Mary Ellen. I want to talk with you."

"Sure, Mary Ellen. You want to meet somewhere?" Marcus knew it would cause tongues to wag if she came up to his apartment.

"No, we can do it on the phone."

"OK. Shoot."

"Marcus, I've been thinking about it a lot, and I want to be a detective."

"You what!"

"I want to be one of your detectives."

"Now where did you get that idea?"

"I've been working on it for some time. I read lots of detective stories and murder mysteries, and I go to all the movies."

"That's impressive, but it hardly qualifies . . . ."

"I know, but I have a good head for detective work. For instance, I can tell you about the case you are working on now."

"And what case would that be?"

"The missing woman over at Zeigler. Several people have told me about it. They say she is the daughter of the head of the coal company. She's some kind of heiress, and she is married to the manager of the mine at Zeigler."

"Not bad." It was about as much as Marcus knew.

"And I saw that rich guy with the chauffeured car go into the court house yesterday. I'll bet he wasn't going in to pay his taxes. He is probably the father of the missing woman."

"OK. So you are observant and you hear a lot of talk at your café—that is not all there is to it. A detective has to get out and investigate—interview people, gather evidence. And let's face it, Mary Ellen—you don't look much like a detective."

"Why not?"

"It's the way you look. You are blond and pretty. Some people think that blonds are . . . well, kind of dumb."

"Do you think I'm dumb?"

"Of course not, but the way you look might be a . . . distraction."

"To whom?"

"Me, for one."

"I could dress more conservatively. I could wear one of my mother's dresses. Heck, I might wear a uniform—maybe even with pants."

"Detectives don't wear uniforms. That's deputies."

"You're afraid people won't take me seriously as a detective because I'm a woman, aren't you?"

"Maybe."

"Well just look at Nick and Nora Charles."

"Who are they?"

"They're the ones in the Thin Man movies. They are both detectives, but all Nick does is drink martinis and act charming. Nora solves all the murders. She's the best detective."

"Look, Mary Ellen, why do you want to do this?"

"I need more excitement in my life. I work at the café six days a week. I close and go home about 2:30 in the afternoon and then I sit around the house for the rest of the evening doing nothing."

"Mary Ellen, you are the prettiest woman in Franklin, maybe the county. Every single guy in town and quite a few of the married ones would like to take you out."

"Oh, I've been through that whole dating thing. Most of the men around here can't carry on a conversation if it's not about deer hunting, baseball, or cars. And all they want to do on a date is get frisky. I don't know how many of them I have had to fight off. I have walked home three or four times."

"There's one more problem. The Sheriff's Department's budget doesn't have any money for a detective."

"I am not asking for a paying job. I'll work in the afternoons and evenings and on my days off—without pay. Don't you have some kind of a sheriff's auxiliary or something like that?"

Marcus thought it over. There was no sheriff's auxiliary, but an elected county sheriff had complete administrative powers over his department. He could do whatever he wanted to with personnel, as long as it did not require more money. If he needed an auxiliary detective without pay, he could create one. But Mary Ellen? What value would she be as a detective? It was true that her café was one of the best places in the county to gather news, probably better than the *Enterprise.* She *did* know a lot of people, and she could provide valuable female insight into the Newcombe case. There was no doubt about her intelligence, and, Marcus confessed to himself, it would not be a bad thing to have Mary Ellen around, not bad at all.

"All right, Mary Ellen, you've got the job. Come over to the sheriff's office tomorrow after you close and I will swear you in. We'll probably go over to Zeigler right after."

"Oh, Marcus! You won't be sorry! I'll be a great detective."

The next morning, Marcus had Sergeant Bailey prepare a departmental memo creating the position of auxiliary detective and another appointing Mary Ellen Selvedge to the position. Bailey could barely suppress a laugh when he first heard about the appointment.

"What's goin' on Sheriff? Is this some sort of joke?" Bailey asked.

"No. It's not a joke. She talked me into it last night."

"Last night, huh. Where was that—out on Pumphouse Road?"

Marcus and Bailey were good enough friends for Bailey to get by with this ribbing.

"No, lunkhead. It was on the telephone. I think she can help with the Newcombe case. So type up the papers and close your trap."

"OK, Sheriff, but I sure would like to have a couple of auxiliary deputies that look like her."

"Look around. Maybe you can find one."

"If I did, she wouldn't match Mary Ellen."

"Probably not."

Early that afternoon, across the street at the City Café, Mary Ellen stood in front of the last lunch customer with a coffee pot in her hand.

"You want anything else, Wilfred? A piece of pie? Coffee?"

Wilfred could not talk because his mouth was full of food. He gulped and finally answered, "Naw, Mary Ellen. I'm nearly finished. What's the hurry? You act like you got ants in your pants."

"Never mind about my pants. But I *am* in a hurry. You sure you don't want anything else?"

"I'm sure. I'll be done here in a few minutes."

While Wilfred finished eating, Mary Ellen cleaned the counter and cleared the grille. When Wilfred paid and walked out the door, she was right behind him. She locked up and headed home to the small frame house on Maple Street where she and her mother lived. She showered and changed into a beige suit with a white blouse and medium heels. When she was dressed, she went to speak with her mother, who was working in the kitchen. She knew the next few minutes would be difficult. Her mother was a very strong person, but Mary Ellen had to make her understand.

Ruth Selvedge looked up from snapping a basket of green beans that lay in her lap. She was a handsome woman with piercing blue eyes and a no nonsense approach to life.

"Well, where are you going—to a wake?"

"Mother, I'm going to the Court House and report for work. When I get there I'll be sworn in as an auxiliary detective in the Sheriff's Department."

Ruth's hands dropped into the basket. "You what? A detective? What on earth are you talking about?"

Mary Ellen sighed. She had thought about this all night. She would just have to be firm. This would not be easy, but she had to keep it on an adult level.

"Mother, you know how I have always been interested in detective stories and movies—it's fascinating! I've always wanted to try to solve a real crime myself. Well, now there is a woman missing over at Zeigler and Marcus has agreed to let me work on the case. I talked with him last night on the phone."

"Marcus—the sheriff? Is that what this is all about? I know you've always been interested in him."

"That's not it at all. I just want to try my hand at being a detective. It's something I really want to do."

"Is it the café, dear? I know it has been hard on you since your father died. Maybe I could help out more—give you some time off."

"I like working at the café. I'm going to keep on doing that. I'll be a detective after I finish at the café. It'll only be part time."

"Do you need more money? Is the café not doing well?"

"No. I'm not getting paid as a detective."

"Then why in God's name . . . ."

"Think about it, Mother. I'm twenty-five years old. All I do is work, come home and rest, eat, listen to the radio, and go to bed. It's not a very exciting life."

"But you have dates, and someday you will find the right man and get married. Then your life will be more interesting."

"That sounds good, but I haven't met the right man yet—not around here. Sometimes I think the only really attractive men are in the movies."

"Mary Ellen, you know those men are not real. They're actors. They have writers for what they say and when they do something awkward or stupid, it just gets cut out of the film. You can't use them as a measure."

"I know that, but what am I supposed to do until Mr. Right comes along? I need more out of life now, not later on."

"I understand that, but what do you know about being a detective? And when you get down to it, is that really a job for a woman?"

"Some of the best detectives are women. Look at Miss Marple in Agatha Christie's books and Nora Charles in the Thin Man movies. They always solve their cases."

Ruth rolled her eyes heavenward. "Oh Mary Ellen, that's not reality. You know that not all cases get solved in real life."

"That's right, but if cases are going to be solved, it stands to reason that there is one quality that is absolutely necessary—intelligence and logic."

"That's two qualities."

"OK—two. So don't you think I have enough of both?"

It was a trap question. Ruth knew that Mary Ellen was both intelligent *and* logical—well most of the time. To deny it would make a false argument and Mary Ellen would know that. To admit it would remove a strong reason for her not becoming a detective.

"All right, Mary Ellen. I can see your mind is made up. I just hope you don't get involved in something really ugly—or dangerous.

She went back to snapping beans. Mary Ellen ran around the kitchen table and kissed her.

As Mary Ellen walked the four blocks to the Court House, she thought about what lay ahead. Her life was about to change. Maybe being an unpaid auxiliary detective in the Sheriff's Department would lead to greater things. If she did well, she might get a full time job, or if she proved to have a real talent for detective work, people might start coming to her to help solve difficult cases. She could even become a private detective, a sort of female Sam Spade. She could open an office in someplace like St. Louis, and . . . .

Mary Ellen tossed her head and smiled. Day dreaming again! It was time to settle down and be practical. If she was going to succeed, she would have to pay attention to everything, take good notes, and listen carefully to what people said and how they said it. Detective work would require using logic and intelligence to put together the pieces of a puzzle. That was obvious. But a successful detective would also need to have a good understanding of people—to be able to tell when they were lying and when they had things to hide, to sense what they were capable of doing.

Mary Ellen suspected that her lack of experience in the real world— after all, she had never been out of Southern Illinois and she had never even seen a dead body—would be a handicap. How could she be sure that what she knew from her reading and the movies would hold up in real situations? Her mother was right about that. Movies and fiction were not real life, and she knew almost nothing about actual crimes and law enforcement.

She slowed her pace as she walked and finally stopped. Maybe this was a bad idea. She could be getting into something that was way over her head. If she was wise, she would turn around, go back home, and phone Marcus to tell him to forget the whole thing.

*No!* She resumed walking. *I'm going to do this. I am not going to let doubts stop me. I'm smart enough to be a detective, and I'll never forgive myself if I back out now.*

Shortly after 2:30, Mary Ellen marched up the Court House steps and into the sheriff's office where Sergeant Bailey sat at his desk. When she saw him looking at her, she said, "What are you grinning at, Orville Bailey?"

Even in her conservative outfit, Mary Ellen was still an eyeful. Her hair was pulled back into a golden twist, and while the beige suit may have concealed some of the curves, there were still plenty.

"Hello, Mary Ellen. How's our new detective?" Bailey said pleasantly.

"I'm not a detective yet. I have to be sworn in."

"OK. The sheriff is gonna do that. He's on the phone now."

When Marcus came out of his office, he was not moving slowly. "That was Newcombe on the phone. He says he has received a ransom note. I'm going over there now."

"What about swearing Mary Ellen in?" Bailey asked.

Marcus looked at Mary Ellen as if seeing her for the first time. "OK," he said.   "Raise your right hand."

She brought her heels together, stood straight, and raised her right hand.

"Do you solemnly swear to uphold the laws of Illinois and Jefferson County?"

She was disappointed at the brevity, but she answered, "I do."

"That's it.   I appoint you auxiliary detective. Have we got some kind of badge, Orv?"

"I've got an old deputy's badge. We'll have to order a detective's badge."

With no further ceremony, Marcus pinned the badge—carefully—on the left breast of Mary Ellen's beige suit jacket. "Let's go," he said as he walked quickly out the door to his car. Mary Ellen came right behind him.

On the way to Zeigler, Marcus went over the pertinent details of the case thus far. Mary Ellen listened quietly, and when he was finished she shook her head.

"Something is not right here, Marcus," she said. "How could Amanda have been kidnapped and now be held for ransom and, at the same time, have packed some of her clothing and other things? And if she was kidnapped, why were there no signs of forced entry in the house and no signs of a struggle?"

"You sure have mastered the detective lingo," Marcus commented. "But I agree. It can't be both ways. I suspect this ransom note may be some opportunist trying to cash in on the fact that she is missing."

"Is that a crime?"

"It's extortion. When we get there, I want to examine that note carefully, and then I want to go out to Newcombe's house and look around some more. I want you to look for things I might have missed the first time—things a woman would know."

Mary Ellen sat back in the car seat and smiled. Now she was a detective.

# CHAPTER 4

When Marcus and Mary Ellen walked into Richard Newcombe's office, Maureen Zalesky was typing, as she had been before. This time her hands froze as she watched them enter.

Marcus breezed past her desk and said, "We'll just go on in, Maureen."

Newcombe's chair scraped as he scrambled to his feet. Marcus quickly said, "This is Detective Selvedge, Mr. Newcombe. Let's see that ransom note."

Newcombe could not take his eyes off of Mary Ellen. He shook her hand and introduced himself. When all were seated, he finally looked away, opened his desk drawer, and handed Marcus a sheet of paper folded three ways. Marcus looked at it and asked, "Was there an envelope?"

"Yes, it came in the mail. I have it here."

Marcus opened the folded paper, read it carefully and handed it to Mary Ellen. He looked the envelope over for almost as long and gave that to her.

The note was written with letters cut out of newspaper headlines and pasted on a sheet of plain paper. It said simply, "WE HAVE YOUR WIFE $25,000 TO GET HER BACK." Naturally, the envelope had no return address, but it was postmarked the day before in Marion, Illinois.

It was addressed in pencil-written block letters to "NEWCOMBE, CONSOLIDATION COAL, ZEIGLER, ILLINOIS."

"It doesn't say anything about when and where you are supposed to pay the ransom, does it?" Marcus said.

Newcombe took his eyes off of Mary Ellen and answered, "No, it doesn't. I suppose that will come later. What do we do now?"

Marcus thought for a moment. "We'll just have to wait. In the meantime, this is enough to call in the FBI. I'll do that when I get back to my office. Do you have the money to pay what they are demanding?"

"No. I can't raise that kind of money. I will have to call her father."

"You had better do that. We may need the money to work with."

"Work with? What does that mean?"

"In order to get her back alive, we may need to let them see the money. I don't intend to let them have it in the end."

"I see. I'll call Chicago right away. Mr. Littleton won't like it, but that amount is not going to bankrupt him."

"Now, I want to go through your house one more time with Detective Selvedge. Please call Mrs. Albagetti, and tell her we are coming. And I'd like to take the note and envelope with me."

When they got in the car, Marcus turned to Mary Ellen and asked what she thought.

"First off, I was getting some strong sexual vibrations from him, not what you would expect from a distraught husband worried about his wife's safety."

"Yeah. He couldn't get enough of looking at you. What about the letter?"

"Not much to go on there. The stationery was cheap stuff, the kind you buy at the dime store. The letters seemed to be pasted on with some sort of homemade paste, maybe flour and water. The font of the cut-out letters suggested the *St. Louis Post Dispatch* to me. Maybe we can compare them. And I'm wondering why they didn't set a time and place to pay the ransom. Also, it's very significant that the sender used the plural pronoun. Either there is more than one of them, maybe a gang, or it was done to throw us off. What do you think?"

Mary Ellen felt she had done well. She looked at Marcus to try to read his reaction. He was looking at her in what she took to be surprise. He turned back to driving the coupe and answered, "Yeah, I think you have a pretty good handle on it." He thought for a moment and then said, "I'm going to send the ransom note and envelope to the state crime lab in Carbondale. Maybe they can get some finger prints off of it. The letter was post-marked Marion. That's about thirty miles south of here. East of there is the territory of the Shelton Gang."

"Then you think it might be the Sheltons?"

"We can't rule them out. It's their sort of thing."

"You mean kidnapping?"

"Yeah, or faking it and trying to extort ransoms."

"I've always heard that the Sheltons are not really very smart, just out-of-work men running around with machine guns and shotguns and pretending they are dangerous."

Marcus turned into the driveway of the Newcombe house. "Oh, they're dangerous all right. They have killed several people, and they are probably responsible for a big part of the robberies and shootings down in Saline and Williamson Counties. And they are suspected of being involved in kidnappings."

He parked next to a new Packard sedan, and they walked to the back entry, where Mrs. Albagetti was waiting for them.

"Hello again, Freddie.  Meet Detective Selvedge. We want to look around some more."

Freddie looked concerned. "Do you think Miss Amanda has been kidnapped, Sheriff?"

"Maybe not, Freddie. That's why we want to look at her room. Have you changed anything?"

"Not since you were here."

Both Marcus and Mary Ellen went over the bedroom and bathroom while Freddie stood and watched. Mary Ellen was most interested in the writing desk and the contents of the locked drawer that Marcus had opened earlier. She sat and read letters and various clippings and papers for half an hour.

Freddie grew tired of standing and sat on the bed. When Mary Ellen was finished she asked, "Did she keep a diary?"

"I don't know. I don't think I ever saw her writing in any kind of a diary, but she certainly could have kept one—she was up here by herself so much."

Mary Ellen found very little that was helpful. She remembered that some of Amanda's clothing was supposedly missing, so she asked to see her closet and dresser. There were house dresses, suits, slacks, blouses, but very few fancy things—nothing that would do for a party or a formal dinner. There was a wool house coat and several cotton wrappers. Amanda's shoes were more practical than dressy.  Mary Ellen's overall impression was of a woman who wore expensive clothes, dressed in good taste, but a woman who was certainly not trying to turn many heads.

"Do you do the laundry?" she asked Freddie.

"Yes."

"Look at this underwear drawer and tell me how much is missing."

Freddie looked and then turned to Mary Ellen in surprise. "There's not much missing—maybe only one or two sets of panties and bras and one slip."

Mary Ellen looked carefully at the underwear.  None of it was lacy or even vaguely sexy.

"How much hosiery or stockings?"

"The same—very little."

"You told the Sheriff that some of her clothes were missing. What do you think it might have been? A dress, a suit, slacks, what?"

"Well, I think it may be a house dress, and maybe a tan suit."

"Shoes?"

"There's at least a pair of oxfords missing."

"Any dress shoes—high heels?"

"She doesn't wear high heels. No, I don't think any dress shoes are missing."

"What about hats?"

"She has several, but they are all still here."

"Where does she keep her make up?"

Freddie showed her the medicine cabinet in the bathroom where there were a few items—face cream, rouge, lipstick, and powder, but little else."

"Does she wear perfume?" Mary Ellen asked.

"No."

All of this fitted Mary Ellen's earlier impression—Amanda Newcombe was certainly not trying to build an image as a high society wife or a glamour girl. She was not even trying to entice her husband. Mary Ellen tried to picture Amanda dining with Newcombe dressed in one of her expensive but plain dresses, none of which were low cut, or coming to say good night to him in the wool housecoat. Small wonder Newcombe listened to baseball games in the evenings or went out to unknown places.

Marcus had grown impatient while Mary Ellen was working, having examined about everything he could think of for the second time. Finally, Mary Ellen said, "I'm finished, Marcus, but I think we should take those coded letters as evidence. We need to know what is in them. Also, we need to get a complete description of Amanda. Surely there must be a picture of her somewhere."

"OK, we'll take the letters, and what about it, Freddie, do you know of any picture?"

"There's an album of wedding pictures in the living room. Has to be a picture of her there."

Naturally, there were several pictures of the bride at the wedding three years earlier. But most of the shots were from a distance, and there were no portraits, so the images were small. Amanda, judging from pictures of her standing next to Richard Newcombe, who was six feet tall, was about five feet six inches. She had dark hair and an oval face. She was slender and rather straight up and down. From the black and white pictures, it was impossible to tell the color of her hair and eyes.

Mary Ellen selected two of the best pictures to have copied and asked Freddie about Amanda's hair and eye color.

"She has light brown hair and brown eyes—yes, I'm sure they are brown, not dark brown but light."

"Well, thanks very much Freddie. We'll be going now," said Marcus.

As they drove back to Franklin, Marcus asked Mary Ellen for her report.

"Marcus, I don't see how Amanda could have been kidnapped. There's no sign of that. And why would kidnappers take some of her clothing, including underwear and a pair of oxfords? She was probably wearing a house dress that day, but she wouldn't have been wearing oxfords with a dress—very poor taste and out of character. She has good taste. She just doesn't seem to want to attract attention."

Mary Ellen hesitated to discuss Amanda's intimate garments, but she knew that to be a detective she would have to get past embarrassment about discussing sexual matters with Marcus.

She forged ahead. "I got the impression Amanda was not even trying to attract attention from her husband."

Marcus wanted to hear more. "Why do you say that?"

"Well, her underwear was . . . um, pretty plain. Nothing lacy or scanty and certainly nothing you could see through.  And if she wore that wool housecoat or one of those cotton wrappers at bedtime, I would imagine she wanted to sleep alone. You would think that a woman married only three years would have some lacy underthings and at least one nice negligee, you know for special . . . . "

"Go on," said Marcus.

"No, I think you are enjoying this too much."

Marcus laughed. "Maybe I was, but what I meant was what else did you conclude? What do you think about the things that are missing?"

"It's strange, but there doesn't seem to be very much of it—maybe a tan suit, but no hat. One thing is pretty sure—she has not just run away. Any woman would have taken more underwear, more changes of clothes and shoes, something to sleep in, and more make-up. And she would have picked things that match."

"Do you think someone tried to make it look like she has run away?"

"If they did, it was probably a man because so little is missing and what is missing seems to be poorly matched."

"What kind of person do you think she is?"

"Well, she is not trying very hard to be attractive. And I don't think she is happily married judging from the separate bedrooms and the other stuff I talked about."

Marcus nodded, "Yeah, Freddie confirmed that to me the other day. What else?"

"I think Amanda is unhappy and very secretive. I'd like to know what those coded letters are all about. I do think they were written by a man, though, judging from the handwriting. And one more thing—she seems to be fascinated by crime and murder mysteries—kind of like me."

"How about her parents? Is she close to them?"

"No. Her letters from her mother were very dull, almost impersonal, and there were no letters from her father. She had quite a few from her sister—her name is Diedra. She's married and lives in Chicago. To tell the truth, her sister's letters were a bit condescending. I got the idea Diedra is a society type and feels kind of sorry for her younger sister."

Marcus drove in silence for a while. Then he said, "You know what, Mary Ellen, we're sure as hell not getting a clear picture here. I'm suspicious of Richard Newcombe, a good-looking up-and-comer married to the boss's daughter, who, it turns out, is a bit mousey and obviously unhappy living  down here in Southern Illinois. Maybe he decided to stage a kidnapping to get rid of her. Or maybe he murdered her or got someone to do it. And to tell the truth, I've been thinking about this—it could be that Newcombe has set this whole thing up—you know, tried to commit the perfect murder."

Mary Ellen said, "Marcus, I've had the same idea. The things that are missing suggest that it wasn't Amanda who selected them. And Newcombe sure doesn't seem to be broken up that she is missing."

"No. He acts like he's a lot more worried about what her father thinks about all of this," Marcus agreed.

But Mary Ellen was not ready to buy the perfect murder theory at this point. "Let's look at it another way. The missing clothes *could* be seen as evidence that Amanda left voluntarily. Maybe she ran off with that past boy friend of hers in Chicago. He may be the one writing those coded letters."

"Could be," said Marcus, "We can't rule that out. And also, we can't really eliminate kidnapping. After all, we have a ransom note. The kidnappers may have been disguised as delivery men and may have come in the house, subdued Amanda, and taken her away without being seen by the gardener. To tell the truth, I am not sure how accurate Freddie is. You say there was very little underwear missing?"

"Yes. She seemed surprised about that."

"Then maybe all that is missing is what she had on— underwear, the house dress, and the oxfords. Maybe she wasn't particular about wearing oxfords with a dress. And the tan suit could be in the cleaners."

"So, where does all of this leave us?"

"The first thing we have to work on is the idea of a kidnapping. I am going to call the FBI as soon as I get to the office."

"What do you want me to do?"

"Write up everything we found out today in a report, and also write up a complete description of Amanda. Then I want you to have Harold Simpson make enlargements of the best photo we have and make a bunch of copies."

"I'll do that first thing so I can catch Harold before he closes his shop."

Marcus went into his office and looked up the number of FBI in East St. Louis, the closest office. He picked up the phone and asked the operator for long distance.

"Federal Bureau of Investigation," a woman's voice said on the line.

"This is Sheriff Marcus Dixon of Jefferson County, Illinois. I need to talk with someone about a kidnapping."

"One moment please."

Almost immediately, a voice said, "Agent Charles Tomlinson speaking. How are you today, Sheriff?"

"I'm fine. I want to report what may be a kidnapping in my county."

"May be? Why do you say that?"

Marcus gave him the whole story, including his suspicions about the identity of the ransom note writers.

"I see what you mean, Sheriff. You may not have a kidnapping at all."

"But we do have a ransom note and the person has been missing for two days. Doesn't that automatically involve the FBI?"

"Yes, the Lindberg Law gives us the authority to enter any kidnapping case after twenty-four hours on the assumption that the victim may have been taken across a state line."

"So what are you going to do in this case?"

"Look Sheriff, we get a lot of missing person cases. Everyone wants to make them kidnapping, but a lot of them aren't. If you had some sign of a struggle or some other way to make it clear it was a kidnapping, we would be down there right away. But right now, all we can do is keep an eye on things. If you will send me the description of the missing person, I will put it on the teletype. That might help."

Marcus read him the description of Amanda on the phone and then had more questions.

"What do you know about the Sheltons? Are they still active?"

"The two brothers have moved up to the St. Louis area, which has always been the market for their bootlegging operation. But we believe that some members of the gang may still be operating in Southern Illinois, particularly at the old Shady Rest. You know about that, I suppose."

"Yes, I know. What kind of activities are these guys into, and do you have any names?"

"Names, no. From what we know, they are into the usual things— prostitution, gambling, slot machines, and there is a steady flow of illegal whiskey coming out of Kentucky and making its way into the St. Louis area. The Shady Rest was always the stopping place for the runners before they came on into our area at night. These guys drive hopped-up cars that can outrun almost anybody. They are also crazy drivers. Have you ever chased one of them?"

"A couple of times. But I never caught one."

"The only car that will catch one of them is a police special. Ford makes a good one."

"Well, a car like that is not in my budget."

"That's the problem. Most of the crimes these gangs are into are local matters. And the sheriffs in those rural counties just don't have the resources to deal with them. As far as we know, no sheriff has ever raided the Shady Rest. I guess that's the reason."

"We do what we can, Agent Tomlinson."

"I know that, Sheriff. At least most of you do. And then there are a few that are . . . well, I won't go into that."

"I understand. Thanks for your help. I'll let you know if there are any new developments that concern you."

"Good, and if I or one of the other agents is down in your area, we will drop by to see how your case is coming."

When Marcus hung up, Sergeant Bailey appeared in his office

doorway and said that Harold Anderson wanted to see him. *This is bad news*, Marcus told himself. He did not want a lot of publicity about the Newcombe case at this point.

"Come in Harold. What's new?"

"That's what I am here to find out. I am hearing all kinds of rumors that the Newcombe woman has been kidnapped. Is it true?"

"We're not sure it's a kidnapping, but as I told you, she is missing."

"Good God, Marcus. This is big news. I've got to publish it."

"I know, Harold, but I don't want a lot of publicity on this right now. If she has been kidnapped, publicity would only make matters worse—much worse."

"How, for Christ's sake?"

"Kidnappers want to operate quietly. If there's a lot of publicity and everyone is looking for them, they'll lay low and not contact the husband. They might even kill her to cover up what they've done."

"Look Marcus, I can't just sit on this story. How would it look if one of those Chicago tabloids gets hold of this and spreads it all over their front page? That's exactly what they may do."

"OK. You can publish that she is missing and that we are investigating."

"What do you have so far?"

"You know I can't talk about that."

"Well, what the hell am I going to say about why she is missing?" Anderson's face was getting red.

"Settle down, Harold. You don't go to press for two more days, right?"

"Yeah. I can insert something that late."

"Then I'll make a deal with you. I'll have some sort of statement about the case day after tomorrow, in the morning."

"All right, Marcus. But this is frustrating."

*You don't know the half of it*, Marcus thought.

Mary Ellen passed Anderson as he was leaving the office. He followed her back into Marcus's office.

"What's going on?" he asked. "Why is Mary Ellen wearing a badge?"

Mary Ellen stood stock still and looked at Marcus.

"She is the new auxiliary detective. She is helping me with the Newcombe case."

Mary Ellen looked at Anderson and smiled sweetly.

"Well, I'll be damned—Detective Mary Ellen. I'll be damned. Can I put that in the paper?"

"It's public information."

"I'll be damned."

"Well, why don't you do your damning somewhere else, and let us get to work," Marcus said.

When he was gone, Mary Ellen laid a stack of photographs of Amanda on his desk and said, "I talked Harold into doing a hurry-up job on these."

Clearly, there were advantages to having a detective as attractive as Mary Ellen.

"Do you have an outfit to wear that would suitable for a date?" Marcus asked.

"Of course, but if you are asking me . . . ."

"No, I'm not asking you on a date—bad policy. Well, maybe I am. You and I are going to look like we are out on a date, and we are going to go check out the Shady Rest."

She gasped slightly. "The Shady Rest! That's a gangsters hideout!"

"No, it's a roadhouse—at least that is what it is supposed to be. I want to go there and check it out."

"And how do you want me to look? A little sleazy? I understand they have prostitution there."

"Do you think you could do that?"

"What? Look like a prostitute?"

"Look a little sleazy."

Mary Ellen smiled. "You don't know much about women, do you?"

"Nope, but sleazy women . . . ."

She laughed. "Right, I'll bet."

Marcus grinned. "OK. We'll go tonight. Be here at 6:30. It'll take an hour or so to drive down there."

"And what are you going to pretend to be?"

"I hadn't thought about it."

"Why don't you try to look like a mobster from upstate? You know, wear a dark suit and black shirt with a white tie, or something like that. And you will have to act tough.  I can be your gun moll."

Marcus looked at her strangely, but Mary Ellen smiled and said, "This is going to be exciting!"

# CHAPTER 5

Marcus made a genuine effort to look like a gangster. He wore a dark suit and black shirt with a cream colored tie. He slicked back his light brown hair with pomade. But he was just not the right type to be taken seriously as a visiting gangster. Mary Ellen, on the other hand, turned herself into a near-perfect blond bimbo. She wore a tight and very short skirt, a low cut blouse, high heels, dangle earrings, and lots of make-up. Marcus hardly recognized her when she walked into the office. Orville Bailey's mouth fell open.

"Will I do?" she asked. "Do I look like a sleazy gun moll?"

"I don't know about that," Marcus observed, "but you look pretty sexy."

"And how!" added Bailey.

"Well, that's the idea, isn't it?" Mary Ellen asked.

"Right. So, let's go," Marcus said, motioning towards the door.

Bailey looked after them, wishing he could be in on this caper.

During the hour drive down Highway 37, both Marcus and Mary Ellen were silent. It was not an easy situation. Neither of them could understand why they had never had a real date before. Finally, Mary Ellen broke the ice. Since they were going to Shady Rest, the notorious roadhouse of the Shelton Gang, she asked, "Marcus, why is it that people around here make such heroes out of criminals like the Shelton brothers and Charlie Birger, especially Charlie Birger."

"You know, I have wondered about that myself. When Birger was hanged in Benton ten years ago, you would have thought that a great man was being martyred. People still talk about it, don't they?"

"I've heard it since I was a girl."

"I guess it's the old Robin Hood business. Birger was supposed to have been a great friend of the people in Harrisburg, even though he was running several gambling dens and brothels. He called himself 'The Protector.' They say he paid for coal for poor families in the winter and wouldn't let local people lose money at his places."

"But he was convicted of murdering several people."

"That's why they hanged him."

"So why is he so idolized?"

"Well, he seemed to be a great guy. He was nice looking, he dressed like a gentleman, he was friendly to everyone, and he died well."

"Died well?"

"You've heard the stories. On the day they hung him, he wore a suit and tie, and he seemed perfectly at ease. He joked with people he knew as he climbed up on the scaffold, and he was smiling when they put the hood over his head. His last words were, 'It's a beautiful world.' And can you believe it, there were thousands of people there to witness the hanging. It was like a county fair."

"There are others like Birger, aren't there—John Dillinger, Baby Face Nelson, Pretty Boy Floyd. The papers are full of them. People make them into celebrities."

"Yeah, they are mostly bank robbers. Before the Depression, bank robbing wasn't such a big thing. But lately, it has become crime number one. I suppose it's true that most people, even though they are desperate and hungry, are just too law-abiding to rob banks. But the same people can sure as hell be fascinated by someone who has the nerve to do it. I guess they think that a guy like John Dillinger is someone you have to admire. At least he's doing something about the Depression—he's robbing banks."

Mary Ellen digested all of this. She had never given much thought to such matters before, but obviously it was important for a detective to better understand what motivated people to commit crimes. Maybe there was a simple explanation.

"Do you think the Depression has caused more crime?" she asked.

"That's the strange part. It hasn't.   Back in the depths of the Depression, when people were going hungry, we didn't have food riots, nobody broke into grocery stores to get what they needed to feed their families, and nobody marched in the streets. The fact is that crime rates went down. You would expect there would be more stealing and drunkenness and that family quarrels over money would lead to more wife beating and child abuse, but it didn't."

"I   guess   Americans   are   just   orderly   people." Mary   Ellen commented.

Marcus nodded. "That's part of it. But I have talked with several people about this. In the really bad days, along about 1932 and early 33, when there were millions of people unemployed and no place to turn for help, folks fell into their own individual depression. They felt helpless. There was nothing they could do to help themselves. So they just sat at home and tried to survive. But they couldn't afford to give up. Maybe tomorrow would be a better day. All of those movies you go to—what are they trying to do? Cheer people up; make them more optimistic about the future. Nobody wants to go to a movie and be further depressed."

Movies. This was an area Mary Ellen understood well. "You're right, Marcus. In the big musicals they're always singing things like *Come on get happy, there's going to be a great day.* " And there's one where Bing Crosby sings about turning your umbrella upside down so you can catch the pennies from heaven."

Mary Ellen was warming to the subject. "And you know—lots of the popular songs are that way. They make you feel good about what you have. The one I like is *My Blue Heaven*. You know how it goes—*'Just Molly and me, and baby makes three. We're happy in my, blue heaven.'*"

"Good example. I guess that sort of thing is working, and, as you say, Americans are orderly people. As long as the government is democratic and is trying to do something about the Depression, Americans will not turn to violence. The simple truth is that they are just not going to riot or overthrow the government because of a damned malfunction of the economy.  What they will do is live one day at a time, making do with what they have. And you know—most of them are too proud to seek a hand-out from the government.  To keep from going hungry they'll work on the WPA. Sure, it's not a real job, and nobody is bragging about being on WPA, but at least it's honest work and it pays a living wage."

Mary Ellen sat silent for a while. She had never dreamed that Marcus was such a thoughtful man. She had always considered him as a decent guy, maybe not overly intelligent, but good-natured and handsome—yes very handsome in an athletic way. To be honest, for some time she had had a mild crush on him, but this Marcus was a whole new person. True, he had gone off to college, but she had always thought that was mostly to be a football player. Now she was seeing that Marcus had an analytical mind and a broad grasp of important things, and he had heart—he could understand the problems of ordinary people.

Marcus turned off of Highway 37 and onto Highway 13. They would soon be at the Shady Rest. "So, tell me about the Sheltons, Marcus. They aren't like Charlie Birger and the others, are they?"

"No, they don't have his style. It's two brothers, Carl and Bernie, and a bunch of their relatives and friends. They got into bootlegging during Prohibition. They're the ones who started Shady Rest. It was supposed to be a roadhouse, and from what I understand, you can still get food there and, of course, now that Prohibition is over, legal drinks. But during Prohibition it was a stop-over for bootleggers running whiskey from illegal distilleries in Kentucky. The market was in the St. Louis area, and they would stop at Shady Rest and wait until dark to make the run on into East St. Louis. They used fast cars, and as the FBI agent was telling me, most sheriffs and town police had no way to catch them."

"So, what part did the Sheltons have to do with it?"

"Apparently, they ran some of the cars, but they also provided food and entertainment for the drivers and a local people. There was gambling, prostitution, cock fights, and even dog fights. None of this stuff was legal, but they were out in the country, right on the line between Williamson and Saline Counties. Neither of the sheriffs in those counties wanted to mess with them."

"Why not?"

"Well, for one thing, the place is like a fortress. The walls are made of logs a foot thick, and there are very few windows. The basement is lined with guns and ammunition and food and water, enough for a siege. There's a high fence around the place and floodlights powered by a generator. One time, during the gang war between the Sheltons and Charlie Birger's Gang, they had an aerial bombing. Birger hired a pilot in a bi-plane to fly over Shady Rest and drop a bomb made of several sticks of dynamite wrapped around a pouch of nitroglycerin. It fell on the barbecue stand outside the place, but it didn't explode. I guess they just didn't know much about making bombs."

"I can't wait to see this place," Mary Ellen said excitedly.

She was not disappointed. Shady Rest did indeed look like a fortress. Flood lights illuminated it and a tough looking security guard stood by the gate as they drove into the parking lot. Mary Ellen took Marcus's arm as they entered the main building. Inside, the smoke was thick and the music from the juke box was loud. A long bar lined the back wall, and around the room were scattered about twenty tables. Along two walls there were booths separated by high partitions. A dozen people, mostly women, sat playing a row of slot machines. The place was filled with people, some drinking, some eating, and a few dancing. An open door next to the bar led to another room where gamblers were shooting dice and playing poker. Behind that, Marcus guessed, was the pit where the cock and dog fights took place.

The entry of Marcus and Mary Ellen caused a stir. Every male eye in the house followed Mary Ellen as she and Marcus walked to a booth. Mary Ellen did nothing to discourage the attention. She moved rhythmically, taking mincing steps in her high heels. The best Marcus could do was to look wary and bored.

A waitress in a sexy dress came to take their orders—two beers and two barbecue sandwiches. The juke box continued to play. Whoever had fed nickels into it liked dance band numbers—Glen Gray, Tommy Dorsey, and Glen Miller. Mary Ellen squirmed a bit in her seat and said finally, "Maybe we ought to dance."

Marcus mumbled something and got out of the booth. He held out his hand and Mary Ellen took it and slid out also. They danced to the mellow sound of Glen Gray and his Casa Loma Orchestra. At first Marcus was stiff, but when Mary Ellen moved close, he began to glide and turn smoothly.

"Marcus!" she said into the hollow of his neck, "you are a great dancer."

He pressed his hand a bit more firmly against her back and brought her closer. "Surprised?" he asked.

"I guess I am."

"There were a lot of dances at the university."

"We should do this more often," she said, trying to make a joke of it.

"Not a bad idea," he added. The way she felt in his arms—no, that wasn't a bad idea at all.

"I'm trying to remember why we are here," Mary Ellen said. "Are you getting any impressions?"

"Well, it doesn't look like any other roadhouse I ever saw. And there are enough tough guys and guys trying to look tough to start a good-sized gang right here. Have you noticed anything?'

"Oh yes. The women in here do not look like anyone's wives."

"Yeah, especially the ones sitting at the bar."

"Do you think some of them are prostitutes?"

"You can bet on it."

The music ended and they went to their booth. They sat sipping their beers when a burly fellow with a bad hair cut who had been sitting at the end of the bar walked to their table. He wore a cheap suit that fitted badly partly because of a suspicious bulge under his arm. .

"Welcome to the Shady Rest," he said without smiling. "Where you folks from?"

Marcus took a drink from his beer bottle. "Up state," he replied.

"Up state," the man repeated. "Where up state?"

"You writin' a book?"

"No. Just curious. We don't get many strangers around here."

"We're traveling through, on our way to Kentucky on a little business."

"And how about you, Blondie? Are you here on business?"

Marcus set his beer down and said flatly, "She's with me. Hit the road."

"No offense, pal."

"I'm not your pal."

"OK. Let's leave it like that. You folks enjoy yourselves."

Cheap Suit returned to the bar, but continued to look in their direction. Marcus stared back and saw another patron at the bar slide down to talk to him.

"This is not good," Marcus muttered.

"Why?" Mary Ellen asked.

"That fellow that's talking to the guy who came over here—I recognize him. I arrested him a few months ago for drunk and disorderly."

Cheap Suit nodded, pushed the bulge in his jacket into a better position and motioned for two other men to follow him as he walked back over.

"So, you're not from very far up state—about one county is guess. I hear you are the hot shot football player sheriff from Jefferson County. What are you doing here?"

"Just out for an evening with my girl friend. You got a problem with that?"

"We don't like lawmen around here, pure and simple. You and Blondie are leaving—now!"

Marcus stood up and faced Cheap Suit. Marcus was four inches taller, and he looked down malevolently. Cheap Suit stared back, but his eyes wavered. Marcus reached for Mary Ellen's hand without taking his eyes off of Cheap Suit.

"Step back," he said coldly. Cheap Suit stood firm for a moment and then stepped back.

Mary Ellen slid out of the booth and they headed for the door.

"The tab is on you, *pal*," Marcus said over his shoulder.

In the car, Mary Ellen said breathlessly, "Oh Marcus! That was sooo exciting."

"I'm glad you liked it."

"And it was scary too. I'm glad we didn't have to fight those three men."

"We?"

"Sure, I was ready to grab a beer bottle."

"Well," Marcus commented, "that would have scared them."

"Oh, be serious."

"Look, we didn't go there to get into a fight, and I think we found out what we needed to know."

"That there are still gangsters at the Shady Rest?"

"Right. And lots of illegal activities."

"Why don't the local sheriffs stop it?"

"They may be in on it, but even if they did raid the place and arrest a few people, it would just spring back up. Also, they may not have a big enough force to make a raid. I'm sure glad it's not in Jefferson County."

"So where do we go from here in the Newcombe case?" Mary Ellen asked.

"What we learned tonight says only that we cannot rule out kidnapping. There are guys hanging around that place—it appeared to be a whole gang of them—who are looking for ways to make money now that bootlegging is over. They might very well be in on the kidnapping of Amanda Newcombe, or they might be trying to cash in on it by sending that ransom note. No, I think we have to keep an eye on the crowd at Shady Rest."

"That won't be easy since they recognized you," Mary Ellen commented.

"Yeah, but the kidnappers, whether they are real or phony, will have to reveal more about themselves when they contact Newcombe again. I expect we will hear from them tomorrow or the next day, and when they do, they are going to have to specify a time and place for Newcombe to deliver the money. If we're lucky, that will give us a clue about who they are. Meanwhile, I want to find out a lot more about two men."

"Newcombe and who?"

"One Hanley Friedman."

"Amanda's one-time boy friend?"

"Yes. Those coded letters are sticking in my mind. Maybe we can get some help from the Chicago police on tracking Friedman down. I'd like to know where he is right now."

"And Newcombe, do you want me to work on that angle?"

"Yes, but keep me informed every step of the way. And be careful around that guy. I don't like the way he looks at you."

Mary Ellen could not tell whether Marcus was jealous or being protective, but either way she liked it.

# CHAPTER 6

Saturday was a day that farm people came to town to shop and to see and be seen. Some came in their old Ford Model A's and Chevys, and some still came in their mule-drawn wagons. Men in overalls and women in cotton print dresses, some made from flour sacks, thronged the business district of Franklin all day long. They visited with friends, exchanged gossip, and window shopped. Very few of them had money to spend on anything but absolute necessities, but still the stores did good business on Saturdays. The same was true of the City Café. Mary Ellen was busier than usual, but she closed at the regular time. She hurried home only a few blocks away, freshened up, and changed into her detective outfit.

When she arrived at the Court House, Marcus was in his office and Orville Bailey motioned her to go in. Marcus looked up from his paperwork and smiled. Last night had indeed been exciting. "Glad you're here," he said. "I've got an assignment for you."

Mary Ellen smiled radiantly. "You want me to go out and catch the kidnappers, right?"

"Something like that. But first, I want you to go over to Zeigler and see what you can learn about Richard Newcombe."

"Has he had another communication from the kidnappers?"

"No, but I think you should go over there and talk with him. Say you have more questions. See what you can find out about his relationship with his wife, and—I've been thinking—Freddie, the housekeeper told me he goes out in the evening sometimes and she didn't know where. I'd like to know what that's all about."

"You're not going?"

"Nah. I've got this paperwork to do, and I am waiting for a call from the Chicago police."

"About Hanley Friedman?"

"Yes. I decided to call the chief of the Consolidation Coal's company police. Randolph Littleton, Amanda's father, offered me their services, and I'll bet a steak dinner he has already had his company police look into Amanda's old boy friend."

"You are probably right, but where are you going to buy a steak dinner if you lose? The City Café is closed for the weekend."

"Guess I'll have to wait." Marcus looked down at his paperwork, but Mary Ellen did not make a move to leave.

Marcus looked up and said, "Oh yeah. That's right—you don't have a car. Do you drive?"

"Yes, but . . ."

"OK, tell Orville to come in here."

Orville came in and Marcus told him, "Take the squad car and drive Mary Ellen over to Zeigler. Stay with her—you can be her partner."

"But what about the office?"

"I can handle things around here. Besides, Hank and Wilford are both on duty in the patrol car. I can get them on the radio."

"OK, Sheriff." Bailey agreed happily. He grabbed Mary Ellen's elbow and said, "Let's go, partner."

Bailey was about 35, slightly balding, big and muscular. He was not a bad looking fellow and had never married. To be sent on a case with Mary Ellen as his partner was a high point in his twelve years as a sheriff's deputy.

On the short drive to Zeigler, Mary Ellen filled Bailey in on what she knew about the Newcombe case, some of which he had read in the reports she and Marcus had filed.

"What do you think so far, Mary Ellen? Who do you suspect?" Bailey asked.

"Orville, I'm new at this. When I read a mystery or see a movie, I can relax and just wait to see how the case is solved. Sometimes, I try to figure out who is guilty before the end of the movie, and it's great fun to be right. But this is different. This is real life. I'm not trying to second guess some writer; I have to determine what really happened. And I have to recognize what is a real clue and what isn't. It's not as easy as I thought it would be . . . but don't tell Marcus."

Bailey nodded agreement, and Mary Ellen was silent for a few seconds.

"But to answer your question, I'm very suspicious of Richard Newcombe. I'm not sure why—it's just a feeling. He just doesn't seem very concerned enough about his missing wife, and they don't appear to have a good marriage."

"So you think he might have had her kidnapped or maybe even killed her?"

"I think it's possible. He wouldn't be the first husband to get rid of his wife by trying to commit the perfect murder."

"Yeah, he could have faked the ransom note to make us think she was kidnapped."

"I think it's more likely that he took some of her things to make it look like she had run off with someone. The ransom note may be a fake, but I doubt if he had anything to do with that. Why would he want to do it? If he had her kidnapped, it would leave the possibility that he would get her back. If he is trying to get rid of her, he wants her gone for good. It's much better for her to have run off with someone. That way she could never be heard from again."

"Sounds like you think he has killed her."

"That's where it seems to lead."

"Then we need to find a body."

"If it is a perfect murder, he will have to find a way to make sure that we don't do that."

"OK. We are about to Zeigler. Where do you want to go?"

"It's Saturday afternoon. The mines are working today, but I imagine the company office is closed. Let's go first to Newcombe's house."

As they walked up the sidewalk to the house, Bailey commented that this must be the biggest and most expensive house in town. "I'll bet there are miner's families living in those four room company houses with seven or eight kids, and there are only two people living in this place."

"And one of them is missing," added Mary Ellen.

Freddie Albagetti answered the door and showed them into the parlor. "Mr. Newcombe is upstairs taking a nap," she told them.

"Please tell him we have a few more questions for him," said Mary Ellen.

When Newcombe came downstairs, his hair was uncombed and his shirt was wrinkled.

"Freddie says you have more questions," he said tiredly. He sat in a chair, crossed his legs, and lit a cigarette, tossing the match folder in an ash tray.

"Yes, this is Sergeant Bailey from the Sheriff's Department. Have you heard anything from the kidnappers?"

"No. I would have called you if I had. What is it you want to know?

"Frankly, Mr. Newcombe, I am puzzled by the indications that your wife took some of her clothing, make-up, and one suitcase with her. That does not square with the idea that she was kidnapped. Kidnappers would hardly allow her to pack her things before they took her away. What do you think actually happened?"

"How do you know what she took with her?"

"Mrs. Albagetti says that is what is missing from her things."

"I see. Well then, I don't know what to think about what happened. Maybe Amanda just left and the ransom note was sent by someone trying to cash in on her disappearance."

"Has your wife ever just up and left before?" Bailey asked.

Newcombe looked at him angrily. "No. Of course not."

Bailey was not deterred. "How were things between you and her?"

"Look, Sergeant whatever-your-name-is, this is not a case of my wife leaving me!"

"We're just trying to determine what happened, Mr. Newcombe."

Mary Ellen tried to ease the tension. "Perhaps your wife has gone off to visit friends or relatives and neglected to tell you about it until later."

"Well, I guess that's possible."

Mary Ellen changed the subject. "Have you ever met a man named Hanley Friedman?"

"You mean the jerk Amanda ran around with before we were married?"

"Yes. Have you met him?"

"Yeah, once. He came here one time—said he had to talk with her."

"Did he?"

"No. I told him to get lost. He's a creep. I don't know what she ever saw in him."

Bailey asked, "Do you think it is possible that your wife might have run off with Friedman?"

Newcombe looked at him evenly. "I have to admit that the thought has crossed my mind."

"The sheriff is checking on Friedman. We'll let you know if we find out anything."

Mary Ellen had one more question. "Does Amanda have any close friends that you know of?"

"None.  I suppose she has friends back in Chicago, but she never talks about anyone like that. As far as around here, she kept pretty much to herself. I'm sure she doesn't have any friends here in Zeigler."

Mary Ellen could not resist saying, "She must have been terribly lonely."

Newcombe did not respond.

As they walked away from Newcombe's house, Mary Ellen asked Bailey what he thought about Richard Newcombe.

"Well, we sure as the devil can't cross him off the list of suspects. He doesn't seem real concerned about what has happened to his wife. Taking a nap on Saturday afternoon—that's hard to believe. If it was my wife that was missing, if I had a wife, I would be doing something to try to find her. I sure as hell—excuse me—wouldn't be taking an afternoon nap."

"Did you notice the match book cover he lit his cigarette with?" Mary Ellen asked.

"No."

"It was about half used up, and it was from Tom's Place."

"Tom's Place. That's a road house over in Jackson County."

"That's right. It's a very popular place to eat, especially for people who don't want to be seen."

"How can they go there and not be seen?"

"They have little individual rooms with doors to the outside. You can dine there and never go through the main restaurant. Nobody will see you but the waiter."

"Have you been there?"

"Once, on one of my dates. I didn't find out until later that the guy was engaged and didn't want his fiancé to know he had asked me out."

"Now that you mention it, I've heard about Tom's Place. It goes back to Prohibition. You could have your bootlegger deliver your liquor at the door to your little room. How was the food?"

"Excellent, until my date started trying to get fresh."

"Did you slap him?'

"Yes."

"Can't blame a guy for trying."

"I suppose not, but it does tend to ruin an evening."

"So what do you make of the match cover?" Bailey asked.

"Well, for one thing, only a few of the matches had been used. That might indicate that Newcombe was at Tom's Place recently, maybe last night. It could be the explanation for why he was taking a nap this afternoon—you know, out very late last night."

"That would be a bit suspicious, wouldn't it?"

"It would depend on who he was out with. He might have been out late at night because he was with someone he didn't want to be seen with."

"So, where do you want to go now?" Orville asked as they got into the car.

"Let's go talk with Newcombe's secretary."

"OK. We'll go by the police station and find out where she lives."

The Zeigler Police Station was a small frame building on a side street off the town circle. Chief Callum was there, and Bailey introduced Mary Ellen to him. "We need to talk with Maureen Zalesky. Can you tell us where she lives?" Bailey asked.

"Maureen? Sure. I'll go along with you. I guess this has to do with the Newcombe Case."

"Right," said Bailey looking questioningly at Mary Ellen. Obviously, being descended upon by three police officers might intimidate

Maureen. Mary Ellen got the point, but there was nothing to be done about it.

The Zalesky's lived in a neat bungalow owned by Consolidation Coal. Alfred Zalesky was not there, and oddly enough, Maureen was taking a nap. It took her five minutes to answer the door. She did so barefooted and dressed in shorts and a man's shirt. She was a very shapely woman, and her saucy brown eyes and pouty red lips framed by rumpled red hair aroused the interest of both men.

"Maureen," said Chief Callum, "these deputies want to ask you a few questions."

"About what?"

"How about we come in for a few minutes?"

"OK, but what's this all about?"

After they took seats in the sparsely furnished living room, Mary Ellen answered. "We are investigating the disappearance of Amanda Newcombe, talking to a lot of people, and we want to know if you can help us."

"How? I don't know much about her. Only met her a few times when she came into the office."

"Did she come to the office much or call frequently?" Mary Ellen asked.

"No. Like I said, I've had very little contact with her."

"Tell us what you can about your boss. Does he make arrangements to meet anyone or go places at night?" Mary Ellen asked.

"How would I know that?"

"You handle his calls, don't you?"

"Yeah, but I don't listen in."

Bailey asked, "Did he make any calls to Tom's Place last week?"

Maureen's eyes wavered slightly. "Tom's Place? I never heard of it."

"It's a roadhouse in Jackson County. We want to know if he was there last night."

"I wouldn't know that."

Bailey bored in. "Where were you last night?"

Maureen stiffened. "What is this? What business is it of yours where I was last night?"

Bailey held up his hands. "It's a police investigation. We have to ask a lot of questions."

"Well, I was here last night. I washed my hair and listened to the radio."

"And what about your husband? Was he here?"

"No, as usual he was down at Hunker's Place drinking beer."

"Is that where he is now?"

"Probably."

Mary Ellen could see there was little more to be gained from Maureen. She was obviously guarded, and quite frankly, she looked like she had had a hard night. "We thank you for your help," she said. "We'll be going now."

"I don't know what help I've given you," Maureen muttered as they left.

"So," Bailey said when they got into the car, "Hunker's Place now, right?"

"Right," answered Mary Ellen.

It was a shock to the patrons of Hunker's when a woman entered their smoky domain. Indeed, the stares of the men sitting at the tables and standing at the bar felt like daggers to Mary Ellen.

Chief Cullum picked out Alfred Zalesky sitting at one of the tables with several other men. They were playing pitch and each had a beer bottle next to his stack of chips. Zalesky was not pleased to see the three officers. He had the same questions his wife had about what they were doing there and why they were asking questions.

Bailey answered him. "We just have one or two questions. Where were you last night, and what time did you get home?"

Zalesky refused to answer. "What the hell is this all about? Am I being accused of something?"

"No," said Bailey, "We're just checking out your wife's story about where she was last night."

"Well, shit. I guess she was home last night."

"You guess? You don't know?"

"She was home when I got there."

"And what time was that?"

"Hell, I don't know—late."

"How late?"

"I said I don't know. One or two o'clock. I had a few beers."

"But you are sure she was there when you got home?" Mary Ellen asked.

"Yeah. I'm sure. Now leave me alone."

On the way back to Franklin, Bailey said to Mary Ellen, "OK, detective, what do you make of all of this?"

"Orville, I think there is a good chance that Maureen was out with Richard Newcombe last night and that they went to Tom's Place. I think that Albert Zalesky was so drunk when he went home, he wouldn't have known if his wife was there or not. And she could have been there, having got back from Tom's Place well before one or two in the morning."

"So," Bailey mused. "It looks like there could be something going on between Maureen and Newcombe, which adds a possible motive for him to get rid of his wife."

Mary Ellen nodded. "You said it yourself. We can't take him off the list of suspects."

# CHAPTER 7

The call Marcus had been waiting for came soon after Mary Ellen and Sergeant Bailey left for Zeigler. Chief Kelly of the Consolidation Coal Company Police was so Irish that he had a bit of a brogue. Marcus assumed he was an old street cop and maybe a former watch commander who had retired early and taken the job with Consolidation.

"So you're wantin' to know something about Hanley Friedman, is it?" Kelly began.

"That's right, Chief. I figure Mr. Littleton alerted you about his daughter being missing," Marcus answered.

"Well, we checked him out a few years ago, when he was romancin' the daughter. He seems pretty harmless. She met him at Northwestern, when they were in college. They were both English majors. He went around lookin' like some sort of poet or something—you know, baggy sweaters and corduroy pants. He even wore one of those Frenchie looking caps with no bill. What do they call them?"

"A beret?"

"Yeah. That's it."

"How long were they a couple?"

"About a year. They went to plays and poetry readings—stuff like that. I guess they saw every museum in Chicago, and that's a lot of museums."

"Did they ever shack up?"

"Nah. We kept an eye on them most of the time. There wasn't even a lot of necking. Mostly, they liked to sit in a park and look kind of soulful, if ya know what I mean."

"I get the picture. So why did they break up?"

"Mr. Littleton broke them up. He didn't want his daughter getting serious with a fruitcake like Friedman."

"Why not?"

"Well, for one thing, he's a Jew, and for another he didn't seem to have any kind of a future. His family has no money, and his highest ambition was to be a poet."

"Did you ever read any of his poetry?"

"Had to. It was a bunch of drivel."

"How did Mr. Littleton break them up—forbid her to see him, threaten to cut off the money, or what?"

"I guess it was both, plus he and his missus pushed Newcombe on her. Invited him to the house, talked about what a fine fellow he was, that sort of thing."

"What do you think of Newcombe?"

"I'd better not answer that. We're getting pretty close to the bone here."

"OK. So can you tell me where Friedman is now?"

"As a matter of fact, I can. He's down in your part of the state. He's got a job teaching English at a CCC camp down there."

"Which one?"

"That I don't know. When we learned he had left town to take that job, we lost interest in him."

"Chief, you've been a big help. Thanks very much."

"You're welcome. I hope you find Amanda. I always kind of liked her. Not flashy but pretty, and not stuck up like . . . well, OK. Let me know if I can be of further assistance."

Marcus was familiar with CCC camps, since there was one in his county. The Civilian Conservation Corps was one of the most popular programs of the New Deal. President Roosevelt had started it in 1933. The basic idea was to take young men between the ages of 18 and 26 from urban families that were on relief and put them to work planting trees and building roads and recreation facilities in national forests and state and federal parks. The pay for the corpsmen was 30 dollars a month, 25 of which was sent home to their families. However, they got free food, clothing, housing, and medical care.

There was almost no downside to the CCC idea, certainly as far as the public and the news media were concerned. The program took young men out of hopeless and unhealthy environments in the cities and put them to work doing constructive things in the clean air of the forests and countryside.

Since there were CCC camps all over Southern Illinois, Marcus needed to find out which one had hired Hanley Friedman. A series of calls beginning at the local congressman's office and ably handled by Christine Phelps, the local operator in Franklin, led finally to the regional office of the CCC in East Saint Louis. A clerk in the office promised to go through the rosters of all the camps in Southern Illinois and get back to Marcus with the name of the camp where Friedman was located. Early next day, the clerk called to say that Friedman was listed as a teacher at the Giant City CCC Camp, a few miles southeast of Carbondale. When Marcus went across the street to the City Café to have a late breakfast, he told Mary Ellen he had found Friedman and was going to drive to the camp right away.

"Can I go?" she asked.

"What about the café?"

"I'll get Mother to come in and take over. She's done it before."

"Sounds good. Be ready in about an hour—I'll pick you up at your house."

It was a good road most of the way to the camp, but the last ten miles or so were a two lane dirt road. To be accurate, because of recent rains it was a mud road. Marcus had driven such roads often, so he negotiated the ruts and bog holes skillfully and avoided getting stuck. They arrived at the Giant City camp about noon. It was named for the strange rock formations in the area. Someone once suggested the formations looked like a city of giants. The area had been heavily logged and was a good candidate for the kind of forest restoration work done by the CCC. It was also on public land, since it had recently been set aside as a state park.

As Marcus and Mary Ellen drove into the camp, they saw several crews of young men working on the roads and building picnic benches and camp sites. They wore the forest green uniforms of the CCC, but many of them had shed their shirts.

"Where are their shirts?" Mary Ellen asked.

"It's a warm day, and they're getting sun tanned. Besides, it's kind of the CCC trademark—lean young men, bare-chested, working in the forest."

"Of course. I remember seeing pictures like that in *Life Magazine*. But most of them are so thin. Some even have their ribs showing."

"They just haven't been eating at the City Café."

"Oh, I'm serious."

"Well, remember. These fellows come from families that are on relief. I guess they haven't been eating well for years."

"It's been rough for a lot of people, hasn't it? When my father died, the only way my mother and I could get by was to take over his café. I had just graduated from high school, so it meant I could never go to college."

"Yeah, it has been rough. I was lucky that I played football. I got a scholarship to the University, which gave me free room and board and tuition for four years."

"I guess we were both lucky."

"True, but I'm sorry you missed going to college. It's a great experience, and you know—you are still college age. Maybe you can go one of these days."

Mary Ellen nodded. She would love to go to college.

They drove past an open area where there were rows of perfectly spaced tents and log cabins.

"This looks like an army camp," Mary Ellen commented.

"Yeah, the CCC camps are run by the U.S. Army. "

"Are they actually in the Army?"

"No. The Army officers administer the camps, and the corpsmen wear uniforms and have military discipline, but they're not in the Army. They are recruited by the Labor Department and their projects are provided by the Forest Service or the Department of Interior."

"Who built the camp?"

"That's a great story. When they set up the first camps, the Army brought the new recruits in trucks to the sites and just dumped them. They gave them saws and axes plus hammers and nails and told them to build their own camp. The Army provided tents, clothing and food. You can imagine the problems the officers had getting organized and teaching those city boys how to build things like log buildings and bridges and roads."

"It looks like they got it done. What is that impressive looking building up ahead?"

Mary Ellen was looking at the nearly completed lodge that sat on a ridge overlooking many miles of what had once been a dense forest. It was a tall building with a steep pitched roof and walls of huge logs and natural stone.

"Let's go in and find someone who can direct us to the office," said Marcus.

He parked the Chevy and they walked up wide steps of ledge stone to enter the building. They passed through massive wooden doors hung on wrought iron hinges and entered a great hall with a two-story vaulted ceiling. They marveled as they looked up at cleverly mortised trusses made of logs and held together with iron straps. Equally impressive was the huge stone fireplace that filled one end of the hall. The floor, which was made of cut ledge stone, was surprisingly uniform and smooth. The roof was supported by columns of tree trunks so big that two men could not join hands and reach around them. The bark had been removed from the trunks, and they glistened softly with varnish. Around three walls of the hall ran a balcony with polished tree limbs for a hand rail. A wide door at the end of the building opposite the fireplace opened onto a dining room lined with windows.

It was a building made from trees cut in the nearby forests and stones taken from creek beds and cliffs in the park. It had been built by amateur workmen with few skills, but clearly an architect, probably an unemployed one from the WPA, had designed it. The stone work was so good that skilled stone masons must have taught the corpsmen. Both Marcus and Mary Ellen looked around in true admiration. The building was a rustic classic, the product of excellent organization and supervision.

"I guess at least some of the New Deal 'make-work' projects turn out pretty well," commented Marcus.

"Some do if this is any indication. What a beautiful building!" said Mary Ellen.

"It's hard to believe that it was built by a bunch of boys with nothing but hand tools." Marcus added.

Through a wide set of doors in the back wall, they could see a crew of workers laying ledge stones on a plaza that looked out over a broad valley. They walked through the doors, and an Army sergeant came over to ask if he could be of help. He directed them to the camp commander's office, which was a frame building back near the tent area they had driven past.

The camp was commanded by Captain William Wedemeyer, who welcomed them in his office. "We don't get many visitors out here, Sheriff," he said looking appreciatively at Mary Ellen. "What can I do for you?"

"We are investigating a missing person, Captain, and we would like to talk with Hanley Friedman."

"Friedman. He's one of our teachers. Is he in trouble?"

"No, but when he lived in Chicago he knew the missing person pretty well."

"I see. If you will have a seat, I'll send someone to get him."

While they were waiting, Mary Ellen asked Captain Wedemeyer what kind of educational program they had in the CCC camp.

"Well, I wouldn't really call it an educational program. Our main job here is conservation work, but many of our corpsmen come from very poor backgrounds. Some of them can't read and write, and many just barely can. So for an hour or two a day, we have classes in remedial stuff such as literacy and basic mathematics. And I mean basic—like grocery store math. Then we have a few classes on things like civics and citizenship. Also, we have training in personal hygiene and sanitation, and we touch on nutrition and personal grooming. You'd be surprised how little some of these young fellows know about these subjects."

"You say they are being taught civics," Marcus asked, "Any danger that they are being indoctrinated politically? You know—are you making New Deal Democrats out of these future voters?"

Wedemeyer laughed. "Well, I suppose there's some of that. The CCC has certainly been accused of doing it by Republicans in Congress. Some of them have even compared the CCC to the Hitler Youth in Germany, but I assure you it is all pretty benign. This is, after all, a very successful and popular New Deal program. I guess we can be forgiven for being positive about it."

"You seem to be pretty proud of what you are doing here," Mary Ellen commented.

"I am."

"Well, that building up there—the lodge—that's something to be proud of."

"Young lady, your great-grandchildren will be able to visit that lodge some day, and they will also be impressed by it."

"What can you tell us about Hanley Friedman, Captain Wedemeyer?" asked Marcus.

"Friedman? He's a quiet fellow. Sticks to himself a lot. He reads books and talks about literature and that sort of thing. He does a good job with his classes—seems to connect with the students, especially the more intelligent ones. I kind of like him. He doesn't cause any problems. Now the other teacher, that's a different story."

"Does Friedman ever leave the camp?"

"Sure, on weekends. Everybody does. We all need to get into town and see the bright lights every now and then. He goes pretty often."

"Where does he go?" Mary Ellen asked.

"That I don't know. There is a train station on the IC down at Makanda. It's only a mile or so walk from here. Lots of corpsmen and staff walk down there every weekend and catch a train. I don't know where they go from there. We also run a truck into Carbondale on Saturday mornings so the corpsmen can go there for the week end. Friedman usually rides on the truck. I think he has been back to Chicago once. He had a week off several months ago."

The office outer door opened and a tall, slender young man entered. He wore a khaki shirt and pants and Government Issue boots, but with his horn-rimmed glasses, pale skin, and worried look on his face, he seemed a sharp contrast to the sun-tanned young men of the Corps.

"Sheriff, this is Hanley Friedman," Captain Wedemeyer said. "And Hanley, the sheriff here and Detective Selvedge want to ask you some questions. You can all go in the meeting room." He pointed to a room close by. They went into the room and sat around a table.

"What kind of questions? What's this all about?" Hanley said nervously.

"We are investigating the disappearance of Amanda Newcombe. Do you know where she is?" Marcus asked.

"Uh . . . Amanda! She's missing? What's happened to her?" He seemed genuinely shocked.

"We don't know. She is gone from her home in Zeigler, and she hasn't gone back to her parents in Chicago. She may have been kidnapped."

"Kidnapped!" Hanley slumped in his chair.

"When was the last time you saw her?" Mary Ellen asked.

"Months ago."

"Where was that?"

"Chicago."

Marcus asked, "Did you ever try to see her in Zeigler?"

Hanley looked up warily. "In Zeigler?" Where she lived?"

"That's right, in Zeigler."

"Yes, I did—once."

"Did you see her?"

"No."

"And you don't know where she is now?"

"Good Lord no."

Mary Ellen asked, "Did you write coded letters to Amanda?"

"Coded letters? I don't know what you mean."

"Letters written in a code."

"No, I didn't."

Marcus stood up. "OK, Hanley, here's my card. If you do hear from her, I want you to get in touch with me immediately."

"I will, Sheriff, I will."

As Marcus drove the Chevy back down the muddy road they had come in on, Mary Ellen was curious why Marcus had ended the interview so abruptly. She remarked, "We didn't ask him very many questions, did we?"

"No, we weren't getting anywhere with him. He was pretty guarded. He wasn't going to tell us anything that we could use. We would have to get him in another setting to really interrogate him properly. What did you think of him?"

She thought for a moment. "Well, he acted pretty surprised and shocked that Amanda is missing. He really loves her—I could tell that.

But he's probably lying about not seeing her when he went to Zeigler, and I'll bet another steak dinner he is the one who wrote the coded letters. We could probably find some coded letters from her in his quarters here in the camp if we searched them."

"There would be plenty of problems getting a search warrant for his quarters in the camp. I don't know what kind of jurisdiction we are in here—federal, state, county, or what. But I don't think a search is necessary. It's practically a cinch he's the one who wrote the letters. What we need to know is how to decode them. We can get copies of the ones we found in Amanda's desk and send them to a decoding expert. I would really like to know what's in those letters."

"So we can't eliminate Friedman from being involved some way in Amanda's disappearance, can we?" Mary Ellen reasoned. "We don't know where he goes on the weekends, we don't know what is in the coded letters, but we do know that he cares about her and has tried to see her since she has been married."

"Right. And I think you are right about him seeing her that time he went to Zeigler and maybe several other times."

"You know, Marcus, he doesn't seem like a very devious fellow, but he is obviously hiding something. I wonder if he is a good enough actor to fake the surprise he showed."

"That's the question, isn't it? If he was faking, he may have been involved in her disappearance, and he may know where she is now."

Mary Ellen stared out the window of the Chevy at the wooded area through which they were passing. *This detective work is not as simple as I thought it would be,* she told herself."

# CHAPTER 8

Richard Newcombe had heard nothing from the kidnappers—nothing in the mail that day, and no phone calls. Feeling stressed and in need of relaxation, he called Maureen into his office and had her close the door. She eyed him suspiciously and kept her distance. She was not about to engage in a bit of desk- top sex in the middle of the afternoon with people coming and going in the outer office.

"Relax, Maureen," Newcombe grinned. "I'm not going to grab you right here in the office. But I sure as hell am tired of this whole mess. I need to get away for a while, at least for an evening. What do you say we go to Tom's Place tonight? Can you get away?"

"Maybe. There's a bully fight this afternoon outside of town. All the good old boys will be there. They'll come back to town afterwards and get drunk in the saloons. They do it every time there's a bully fight."

"Bully fight. What's that?"

"Oh, it's a big deal around here. Every town has a bully fighter. I guess it started out that he was actually the town bully. Then, someone from one town told someone from another town that their town bully could whip the other town's bully—you know, like two kids saying my dad can whip your dad. So now we have bully fights between the champion bully fighters of each town. It's kind of like high school football games between towns. Zeigler's bully is Pete Zalesky. He's one of Al's relatives—some kind of cousin I think. He's big and dumb and mean, very mean, and he usually wins. He's fighting the bully from Herrin. It's a big fight. Al will sure be there."

"And they'll all get drunk after?"

"They'll all get drunk at the fight, and then they'll come back into town and have an all night drunk. The winner buys drinks."

"So Al will not be home until very late."

"That's right, but there's a problem with going to Tom's Place. The sergeant from the Sheriff's Office and that kewpie doll detective asked me a bunch of questions about that place in particular—did I make reservations for you there, where was I the night before, stuff like that."

"What did you tell them?"

"I told them I never heard of Tom's Place, but do you think it's a good idea to go there tonight?"

"We can get one of the private rooms. No one will see us, and besides it's the best place to eat around here."

"OK, I'll call over and reserve a room, but we can't stay all night in the motel. That's pushing it."

Newcombe placed his hands on her hips and drew her to him. "We don't need all night," he whispered as he moved to kiss her.

Maureen squirmed away and headed for the door. "Later," she laughed. "Pick me up at the corner as soon as it's dark, and make sure no one is around to see me get into the car."

Oddly enough, Marcus and Mary Ellen decided to check out Tom's Place on the way home from the Giant City CCC Camp. It was only a few miles out of the way, and they were hungry. They got there before dark and parked in the small parking lot that surrounded the building. Tom's was a T-shaped two story building. The dining room was in the long part of the T and the entry was in the east end of the short part. Marcus and Mary Ellen walked into the entry way and quickly spotted a bar alcove to the right.

"Would you like a drink?" Marcus asked.

"Why not, we're off duty now, aren't we?"

"Well, sort of. But a drink sure won't hurt anything."

The bartender wore a white jacket and the back bar behind him displayed an impressive array of whiskies and liqueurs. The restaurant was softly lit and tastefully furnished. The décor featured pictures of trotting horses, suggesting that many of the patrons of Tom's Place were connected to the well-known race track at the DuQuoin State Fair Grounds only a few miles up the road. The track was on the national harness racing circuit. It was a matter of local pride that the biggest harness race of the year, the Hambletonian, took place there every August.

When she was asked what she wanted to drink, Mary Ellen remembered the last Thin Man movie she had seen. Nora Charles drank martinis just as Nick did, and in some of the films she even got a little tipsy.

"I'll have a double martini, please—very dry." Mary Elllen had never had a martini in her life.

Marcus looked at her questioningly. "You sure?"

"Why, yes. Why not?"

"Two double martinis," Marcus told the bartender, who nodded with a knowing smile. These two were going to have fun tonight.

Mary Ellen watched with fascination as the bartender mixed six ounces of gin and precious little vermouth in an ice-filled metal shaker. He stirred the mixture gently and poured it into two iced martini glasses, holding back the ice with a wire ring. Then he ceremoniously dropped a medium-sized Spanish olive into each glass.

Mary Ellen was amazed. "It's not very big, is it?" she commented.

"No," said Marcus, "but watch out for it." He lifted his glass to hers and they clinked. "Here's to successful detectives," Marcus toasted.

Mary Ellen tasted the martini and rolled her eyes heavenward. "My goodness. That is quite a taste!" She took another sip.

"Sit right here while I go check on eating arrangements," Marcus said.

"Oh, yes. I'll do that," she said as she raised her martini glass to him.

A middle aged man in a dark suit and with his hair slicked back stood behind the stand at the entry to the dining area. Marcus asked him for a table for two.

"Did you want a private room?" he asked.

"No, out in the dining area will be fine." Marcus hoped to be able to see into some of the private rooms when the doors were opened by the waiters. He decided to quiz the maitre d'.

"One more thing, Mr. . . ."

"Smithson, John Smithson,"

"OK, Mr. Smithson. Do you know a man named Richard Newcombe, and does he ever come in here?"

"No, Mr . . . . uh—He looked down at his reservation list . . . Dixon. We never give out the names of our patrons. You can be sure you will be afforded the same courtesy."

Marcus knew that if he mentioned being a sheriff involved in an investigation, he would get the same answer.

When he got back to the bar, Mary Ellen had finished her martini. Her eyes were shining.

"OK. We've got a table in the dining room."

"Aren't we going to have another drink?" she asked mischievously.

"We'll have one at the table."

"Great! Let's go."

The dining room was also tastefully done with linen tablecloths, fine china and silverware. All of the doors to the private rooms, which lined the long west wall, were closed except for one where a waiter was setting the table. From where they sat, Marcus and Mary Ellen could see that the rooms were indeed private. In fact, they were so small that with four people seated, a waiter could not move all the way around the table. A door at the back of the room opened to the outside parking lot. At the far end of the dining room, a dark-haired fellow in a tuxedo played popular tunes, occasionally reaching for a glass of whisky that sat on his piano. Tom's was a fancy place, but it was still a roadhouse.

Marcus ordered two more martinis, not doubles, and examined the menu. He had a steak and Mary Ellen chose a broiled chicken dish. They had a fine meal and talked quietly about their day, the CCC, and the case in general. Both tried to look into the private rooms when the food was served, but the waiters never opened the doors wide enough to see much. Half way through the meal, a waiter came and closed the door of the one private room that was open.

After desert, a slice of cheese cake topped with an apricot sauce, Mary Ellen looked around their pleasant surroundings. "Have you ever seen *Roadhouse*?" she asked.

"If that's a movie, I haven't seen it."

"It's about a roadhouse a lot like this one, even with a piano player.

It stars Ida Lupino and I can't remember who else, maybe Humphrey Bogart. Anyhow, the piano player sings this great song.  She began singing softly:

Quarter to three.

There's no one in the place
except you and me.
So set 'em up, Joe.

Got a little story
I think you should know.
We're drinkin', my friend,

To the end of a sweet episode.
Make it one for my baby

And one more for the road.

"That was good, Mary Ellen," Marcus said appreciatively. "Would you like one more for the road?"

Her only answer was a beautiful smile.

As they drank their one for the road, waiters began taking drinks and food to the private room that had been open earlier. Marcus remarked, "I would sure like to know who is in that room."

"So why don't we just go over and open the door?" Mary Ellen suggested.

"See that big fellow sitting by himself in the corner. He's been drinking that same beer for half an hour. My guess is it's his job to see that no one does what you just proposed."

"Oh—still, it might be fun."

"I'm going to have to quit bringing you to places like this. And speaking of that, it's time for us to go."

When they got in the Chevy, Marcus turned on the lights and cruised around the parking lot looking at the parked cars. He stopped and backed up to look at a late model Packard sedan. "That," he said triumphantly, "is Newcombe's car. I remember seeing it at his house, and the license plate was issued in Jefferson County."

"What are we going to do?" Mary Ellen asked.

"We need to know who is with him. We'll just park over there under that tree and wait to see who comes out."

A full moon had risen in the east, a huge golden ball on the horizon. Soon the parking lot would be flooded with moonlight, so Marcus' choice of a place in the shadows to wait was a good idea. They parked and settled back in their seats. The drinks and good food made them mellow. Ten minutes passed, and no one emerged from the private room.

"Marcus," Mary Ellen said finally, "have I been any good as a detective? I know it was a crazy idea, and I talked you into it, but is it working out?

"You've only been on the job a few days—too early to tell."

Not the answer she wanted. "Haven't I helped some?"

"Sure you have. You have asked good questions, and you certainly have a different slant on things. Yes, you have helped."

"People are going to talk about us, you know—running around together, supposedly on sheriff's business."

"Let 'em talk."

"That's what I say."

She moved close to him, laid her head on his shoulder and went to sleep. Marcus sat watching the private room doors and thinking about everything. He wanted to put his arm around her. The scent of her hair was wonderful, and her soft body against him was enough to take his mind off of the business at hand. He was not sure where working with Mary Ellen was leading, but he didn't care.  He knew one thing for sure—he liked having her around. She was not only a pleasure to look at, she was good company—pleasant and intelligent.  No denying she had some good ideas about the case. Yes, it was good having her around.

The door to the private room came open and a man and a woman walked toward the Packard. "Wake up Mary Ellen," Marcus whispered. "They're coming out."

She was awake instantly. "Can you tell who it is?"

"It's Newcombe and Maureen Zalesky."

"His secretary? Are you sure it's her?"

"Yep. It's her."

"How can you tell? I can't. I only saw her that one time."

"I used to go with her. That's Maureen."

"You used to go with her! Why didn't you tell me that?"

"It was several years ago, before she was married."

"Well how can she go out with Newcombe if she is married?"

"Beats me. Her husband is a pretty hard drinker. Maybe she gets home before he comes in, or maybe he just doesn't care. Maybe he has a girl friend."

"Nice people. So where does this leave us?"

"I think it adds weight to the idea that Newcombe may be involved in Amanda's disappearance."

Next morning, both Mary Ellen and Marcus were tired from lack of sleep, but both were on the job at the usual time. Marcus was not surprised to see Harold Anderson, editor of the *Enterprise,* waiting in his office when he came down from his apartment. Anderson was anxious: "Sheriff, you promised me a story. I'm holding up running the paper today to put it on the front page."

"OK, Harold. You can say that Amanda Newcombe, wife of Consolidation Coal manager Richard Newcombe and daughter of Randolph Littleton, owner of Consolidation Coal, has been missing since last Tuesday. The Sheriff's Department is investigating, and since she may have been kidnapped, the FBI has been notified."

"May have been kidnapped? Why do you say that when there's a ransom note?"

"Because there has been no further communication from the supposed kidnappers. We think the original note may, and I emphasize *may,* have been an attempt to extort money from the family by someone pretending to be the kidnappers."

"You keep saying kidnappers, plural."

"The note used the pronoun "we.""

"Is that all? What else has your investigation turned up?"

"I've told you all I can at this point."

"Is the FBI going to come in on the case?"

"Not yet."

"I'll bet they do when this hits the Chicago papers. Have you got a picture of her?"

Marcus gave him a print of Amanda's wedding picture.

Anderson looked at it for a moment. "Good! She's pretty." He started out the door but turned to speak. "Marcus, I'm going to run this story and put it on the AP wire. This is big. The Hearst and Pulitzer papers will eat it up. It'll go national. You can expect to see a bunch of reporters down here in short order."

Marcus groaned. *Just what I need—a bunch of big city reporters crawling all over the place!*

# CHAPTER 9

Harold Anderson had been accurate in predicting that the Chicago newspapers would make a big story of the disappearance of Amanda Newcombe. The early editions arriving by train in Southern Illinois in the afternoon carried 32 point headlines proclaiming "COAL HEIRESS KIDNAPPED" and "DAUGHTER OF CHICAGO INDUSTRIALIST MISSING." The stories had only the facts from the AP wire story that Anderson's had filed, but true to the tradition of the Chicago dailies, they added considerable lurid speculation about what may have happened to Amanda. The St. Louis newspapers also picked up the story and treated it much the same way.

When Marcus came down to his office that morning, the telephone was already ringing. Reporters were calling from both cities seeking more details and new developments. Harold Anderson was camped in the office waiting to talk with Marcus.

"Anything new?" he asked anxiously as Marcus entered.

"Nope. We're still investigating. I'll let you know when there is something. No need to hang around here."

Anderson left grudgingly.

"What *did* you turn up yesterday, Sheriff?" Sergeant Bailey asked.

"We tracked down Hanley Friedman. He claims to know nothing about where Amanda is. And on the way back, we stopped by Tom's Place. Guess who we saw there?"

"Newcombe?"

"Yeah."

"And who was he with?"

Marcus poured himself a cup of coffee. "Would it surprise you to know it was Maureen Zalesky?"

"No, that's not a big surprise. He has a reputation for being a skirt chaser. You used to go out with Maureen, didn't you?" Bailey grinned slyly.

"You saying I'm a skirt chaser too?"

"Well, you did kinda have that reputa . . . ."

"Never mind, Orville."

The phone rang and Sgt. Bailey went back to business. He answered the phone and looked up quickly. "It's Newcombe."

Marcus went into his office and picked up the phone.

"I've got another letter from the kidnappers," Newcombe reported.

"What does it say?"

"I'll read it: 'PUT $25,000 IN RR 3 BOX 243 MARION.' What should I do?"

"Don't do anything right away. We'll be over there in an hour."

Marcus left Bailey to deal with the phone calls and walked across the street to the City Café. Mary Ellen was busy, but she was not as bright-eyed as usual. Marcus ordered breakfast and told her he was going to Zeigler. She phoned her mother and asked her to come in and take over the grille so she could accompany him.

Back at his office, the phone rang just as Marcus walked through the door. It was a call from FBI Agent Charles Tomlinson. *Now they're interested. He must have read about it in the St. Louis papers,* Marcus told himself.

"What's new in the Newcombe case, Sheriff?" Tomlinson asked.

"Newcombe received a letter demanding money."

"That's it then. The FBI is going to enter the case. It'll take me two or three hours to get there. I would like to see the letter and talk with Newcombe. I'll come to your office, and we can go see him together."

"OK. I'll be here."

Marcus phoned Mary Ellen and told her they had more time and probably would not go to Zeigler until early afternoon, which suited her well. He also phoned Newcombe.

Agent Tomlinson arrived shortly after 1:00 o'clock. He was middle-aged and just about medium everything—height, weight, brown hair, dark suit, and conservative tie. His only striking feature was nearly black eyes that had a dull shine and seemed to take in everything. Marcus briefed him on the investigation thus far and then asked him if he had eaten yet.

"No. Why?"

"My auxiliary detective runs a café across the street. She will close it in about half an hour, but we can get a quick lunch before she does. That way she can go with us to talk with Newcombe."

Tomlinson was accustomed to dealing with the leisurely pace of police work in rural counties. "Suits me. Sheriff," he agreed. "I hate to interview anyone on an empty stomach."

Tomlinson did a classic double-take when he first saw Mary Ellen. "She is your detective?"

"That's her. She's part time. I don't have a big enough force to have a regular detective."

Marcus could guess what was going through Tomlinson's mind. He probably suspected some sort of hanky-panky between the young sheriff and a female detective who was as pretty as Mary Ellen. *Well, let him think what he wants; I like having her on the case.*

Marcus introduced Tomlinson to Mary Ellen and explained the plan. She fixed them both a quick lunch, shut the grille down, and locked the door. As they finished their lunches, she took off her apron, straightened her hair a bit, and came to sit with them. "I'm ready to go," she told them. Tomlinson nodded. He was rapidly developing an attitude much like Marcus's—it was nice to have her around.

When they met with Richard Newcombe, he was visibly upset. "I talked with Mr. Littleton on the phone. He wants me to pay the $25,000—anything to get Amanda back. He's very angry."

"Who's he angry at? Marcus asked.

"It seems to be me."

Agent Tomlinson reassured him. "That's natural Mr. Newcombe. He needs to be angry at someone, and you are the only one at hand."

"What should I do? I've got the money. Mr. Littleton sent it by wire."

Tomlinson answered, "If you pay them now, you may never see your wife again. They might kill her just to prevent her from identifying them. What we need to do before you pay any money is determine if they really have your wife."

"How can we do that?" Newcombe was beginning to whine.

"Well, let's think this through. They want you to put the money in a rural route mail box. It must be a very special box, one that they can watch around the clock and one that they can get the money out of without being seen. I think we need to talk with the rural mail carrier of Route 3 and find out more about that box."

"But how is that going to tell us if they have my wife?"

"Instead of giving them money, we will put a note in the box telling them they must prove that they have her before you pay anything."

Newcombe pulled a sheet of paper from his desk and reached for a pen. "OK, tell me what to say."

"Just say, 'PROVE YOU HAVE HER.' Let them figure out how to do it."

Marcus added, "We need to get down to Marion right away and be there when the mail carrier comes in off of his route. That will tell us something about this 'special' mail box. We can let the carrier put the note in the box tomorrow when he runs his route."

Mary Ellen, who had been listening carefully, observed, "It's obvious that these people are able to watch the mailbox. As you said, Agent Tomlinson, they would have to have a plan to get the money out of the box without being seen, probably at night, but they would also need a plan to intercept anyone who stops and gets in the box during the day, before they can get to it. Also, since they can see what is put in the box, don't you think it should look like a packet of money, not just a letter or note. Otherwise they might not risk trying to get it out."

Tomlinson looked at her appreciatively. "Right. You are both right. We will cut up some paper the size of bills. Twenty-five thousand in small bills is a sizeable stack of money. We'll put the note on top of the stack and wrap it in a package."

Newcombe had recovered his composure. "Why don't I just write them a check?" he quipped.

"This is no time for jokes, Newcombe," Tomlinson warned.

Mary Ellen stared at Newcombe, trying to interpret his sudden mood change, but he was busy brushing something off of his lapel.

"All right," Marcus interjected. "As soon as the fake money package is ready, we had better head down to Marion. We will have to alert the sheriff of Williamson County and get him to cooperate. I have no jurisdiction there."

Sheriff Alvin Braxton of Williamson County already knew about the missing coal heiress, and he was quite willing to cooperate. He offered two of his deputies to assist in the operation to plant the false payoff in the rural mailbox. After Marcus, Mary Ellen, and Tomlinson talked with Braxton, their next stop was the Marion post office. It was 3:30 in the afternoon, and the postmaster said the rural route carrier for Route 3 would soon be in from running his route.

The carrier's name was Will Smith. He had a shock of white hair and a deep sun tan, but typical of rural mail carriers, his right arm was much darker than the left. In the summer, car drivers rode with their left arm on the window sill on the driver's side of their car. That made it easier to make the arm signals required by law. It also made the left arms of many drivers darker because they got more sun. But rural mail carriers drove on the right side of their cars, so their right arms were darker.

Will Smith had the appearance of a man who had been carrying the mail for more than a few years. Marcus explained the situation to him and asked, "What can you tell us about Box 243?"

Smith did not have to think very long. "Oh yeah, I get it. That box is completely isolated. It sits on a dirt road that runs through a forest. There's an abandoned house back in the woods, but the box is not used anymore. The thing is, no one can see that box when something is put in it."

"That's why the kidnappers are using it," Agent Tomlinson said. "They probably have someone hiding in the woods and watching it during the day. If they see something put in the box, they will assume that somehow we are watching it also, so they will wait until night to get the package."

"So now we have the question of who will make the drop. How

about you, Mr. Smith? Would you be willing to deliver our package like it was part of the mail?" Marcus asked.

Will Smith, for all of his sixty-one years, had a spirit of adventure. "Tell you what," he answered, "I'll do it. I pass that box every day. I'll put your fake pay-off package in there for you."

"There might be some danger, Mr. Smith," warned Tomlinson.

"Hell, life ain't no fun if you don't take a chance now and then," Smith answered.

They gave him the fake money package and then went back to Sheriff Braxton's office to make a plan for the next day. "I think we ought to try to take these guys down when they come to get the money," Tomlinson began.

Marcus was surprised. "Why? If we catch one or two them, they will still have Amanda hid out somewhere. It won't free her."

"And they might kill her then in desperation," Mary Ellen added.

"Yes, but if these guys are bluffing, if they really don't have her, when they see the note demanding proof, they will know the jig is up. They'll drop the whole thing then, and that means they will be getting away with extortion. We don't want that. On the other hand, if they do have her and they are able to send Newcombe some sort of proof, we will be in exactly the same situation we are now. We will have to deliver the money, probably to the same mail box, and our only course of action will be to try to take them down then. Either way, our best bet to get the woman is to capture one of the suspects and interrogate him to find out where she is."

"Interrogate? What makes you think one of them would talk?" Marcus asked.

"Look. These guys are kidnappers. Under the Lindberg Law, they're facing the death penalty if they are convicted. A good interrogator can get one of them to roll over on the others just to save his own hide."

"But the Lindberg Law applies only when the victim is taken across a state line. It takes that to make it a federal case." Mary Ellen had seen a movie with just such a situation.

Tomlinson turned to the two sheriffs. "Don't you have a baby Lindberg Law in Illinois?" he asked.

Both nodded yes. It meant there was a Lindberg law that applied within Illinois. Braxton added, "And the penalty is the same—death."

"All right, then are we agreed to try to set a trap for them tomorrow?"

Everyone nodded.

"Let me lay out a plan," Tomlinson began. "We'll have to have someone in position to watch the mailbox during the daylight hours. That someone will have to be hidden in the forest and will have to be armed in case he is discovered. The kidnappers will also have someone hidden and watching the box. If their lookout sees something put in the box during the day, they will try to retrieve it that night. It may be the lookout guy, in which case he will have to make his way to a car that is hidden back somewhere in the woods. The other possibility is that one of the gang will just drive by in a car and get what's in the box. Either way, we have to try to catch them before they get away."

"The guy in the woods will be the hardest," Marcus reasoned. "He can just melt back in there and be very hard to follow. His hidden car could be anywhere."

Sheriff Braxton interjected, "Not necessarily. That is a pretty dense forest with very few roads. Actually, there's only one other road anywhere near that mail box. It runs sort of parallel about a mile away and eventually joins the main road farther down toward town. It's just a dirt lane, used mostly by loggers."

"Excellent," said Tomlinson. Then all we have to do is block both ends of that road, and we'll have a good chance of catching them when they try to leave."

"And we can do the same thing on the road where the mail box is," Marcus added.

"Yes, but all of this is going to call for quite a few officers and some coordination. Sheriff Braxton, I assume you have radios in your cars—and you too, Sheriff Dixon?"

Braxton answered first. "I've got two cars you can use. They have radios."

"I have two also, with radios," Marcus answered.

"Can they all communicate with each other?

"Yes," Braxton answered. "We have communicated with Jefferson County before, but these radios have a short range. We'll need some sort of central station near the scene."

Tomlinson thought for a minute. "We'll probably be able to use the radio in my car for that purpose. It can be tuned to different frequencies. I also have a hand-held radio that will communicate with my radio, but not the others."

And so the details were worked out. Sergeant Orville Bailey was to be the spy in the woods. He would be dropped off by a car a quarter of a mile past the mail box and make his way back through the woods to find a hiding place where he could watch the mailbox. He would be armed and have the hand-held radio. If someone came to pick up the package in the mailbox, he would radio to Tomlinson's car which would be hidden off of the main road about half a mile away. Mary Elllen would be in Tomlinson's car to operate the radio. Sheriff Braxton would have two cars hidden in position at either end of the forest road, and Marcus would have two cars with his deputies hidden on the main road about a half mile away on either side of the mail box. When Bailey reported by radio that someone had picked up the package, Tomlinson would coordinate what was done next. If the pick-up was made by a car, Marcus's two cars would block the road and Braxton's two cars would come to their aid. If the pick-up was made by a man on foot, the opposite procedure would be used. In any event, Braxton's men were to block both ends of their road as soon as it was dark.

Mary Ellen could only marvel at the neatness of the trap. "This is going to be so exciting," she exclaimed. The two sheriffs and the FBI agent looked at each other, slightly dismayed. Tomlinson said what was on all of their minds: "If this is the Shelton gang or someone like that, things may get a lot more than exciting. Those guys' favorite weapon is a Thompson sub-machine gun, and they love to spray the damned things around. Let's just hope this works without a big fire fight."

# CHAPTER 10

Will Smith picked up Sgt. Orville Bailey about three miles before his mail route brought him to the now infamous Box 243. Since Bailey was going to be the spy in the woods, he was well armed with a shotgun and pistol and the hand-held FBI radio that would communicate with Agent Tomlinson in the control car. He even had a couple of sandwiches provided by Mary Ellen. Bailey lay out of sight on the floor of Will Smith's Model A Ford when Smith put the decoy package in Box 243. Then, when the Model A was well past the mail box and around a curve, Smith stopped and let Bailey out of the car. The sergeant carefully worked his way back through the heavy woods until he was in a well hidden position where he could watch Box 243.

Meanwhile, four cars, each with two officers, took up the planned positions on the main road and the forest road. Agent Tomlinson and Mary Ellen were parked out of sight up a country lane off of the main road. All was in place. There was nothing to do now but wait. No one knew how long they would be there, and the tension of waiting wore on everyone's nerves.

Tomlinson was not happy to have Mary Ellen for a partner. He was afraid she would be a liability if there was shooting, and he was even less happy about having responsibility for her safety. She had, however, been in on the case from the beginning, and Sheriff Dixon had made it clear she was part of the operation.

Mary Ellen was uneasy also. She sat, a bit stiffly, next to Tomlinson in his car. When the agent asked if she was armed, she answered, "No, I talked with Marcus about it, and he said that since I have no training in firearms, I shouldn't be armed."

"I don't agree," said Tomlinson. "If push comes to shove, you might have to defend yourself. And you sure as hell would be a sitting duck without a weapon.  Here, take this."

He pulled a .38 caliber Colt service revolver from the glove compartment of his car, flipped the cylinder out and unloaded the six cartridges. Then he showed her how to cock and aim the pistol, using both hands, and how to make a steady pull on the trigger.  He had her practice aiming at trees and bushes and pulling the trigger. Finally, he declared her ready for action. He loaded the Colt and handed it to her butt first. "Here," he said, "you have six shots. I hope to God you don't need them."

Mary Ellen took the loaded pistol gingerly. It might have been a ticking bomb. "Where shall I keep it?" she asked.

"Put it in the glove compartment and don't take it out unless you have to."

They sat without talking for twenty minutes—it seemed much longer. The silence of the forest was oppressive. Finally, Mary Ellen spoke. "Have you ever shot anyone?" she asked.

Tomlinson frowned. "Yes."

"In the line of duty?"

"It's the only way to do it."

"Did you kill them?"

"No—wounded him badly. He's crippled now."

"Who was it? A bank robber or a murderer?"

"We don't deal with murderers much. That's a state crime. It was a bank robber."

"What was he doing when you shot him?"

"Shooting at me."

"What did you shoot him with?"

"That's enough questions. I've got a few for you. From the beginning I've been wondering why you want to be a detective.  Shouldn't you be back in Franklin taking care of your café?"

"Would you want to be a fry cook the rest of your life?"

"Well . . . I suppose not."

"I don't either. I want to get more out of life than that."

"How about getting married and having a family? What's wrong with that?"

"Nothing. I want that. But it has to be with the right man."

"How about Marcus? You two seem attracted to each other, and you could have some great looking children."

That was about as far as Mary Ellen wanted to go with this subject. "Agent Tomlinson," she said, "You're getting into a pretty sensitive area. Let's talk about something else. Do you have a family?"

"That I do. A wife and three kids. The oldest is ten."

"Does your wife worry about you being in the FBI—the danger and all?"

"Yeah, I guess she does."

"So why don't you get a safer job?"

"Now you are getting into a sensitive area."

"I'll bet the answer is that you like this kind of work."

"OK. Let's talk about something else."

They did. They discussed the case from every angle. Tomlinson doubted if the supposed kidnappers really had kidnapped Amanda. He didn't think they were behaving like most kidnappers. Mary Ellen had the same suspicion, and hearing Tomlinson express it only strengthened her feeling.

Night came and Mary Ellen began regular radio checks with the four squad cars. She did not use the hand-held radio that Sgt. Bailey had for fear the sound would reveal his position. The moon had not risen yet and the night was dark. The only sounds were those of the forest—the eerie *hoo hoo ha ha haw* of owls calling to each other, the croaking of tree frogs, the rustle of feeding deer. Occasionally the lights of a passing car or truck moved along the main road, barely visible through the thick forest.

Hours passed. Mary Ellen and Tomlinson had long since quit talking. They sat in complete darkness except for the faint light from the dial of the two-way radio. Tomlinson grew restless and leaned forward to adjust the radio dial. Just then, there was a flash as a .38 caliber slug ripped through flesh and bone below his right ear and crashed into the floor board. Mary Ellen screamed and lunged for the pistol in the glove compartment, but a strong arm reached through the window and pulled her roughly out of the car. She felt the barrel of a pistol pushed against the side of her head.

"One peep out of you sister and I'll blow your brains out," a gruff voice muttered. On the other side of the car, the man who had shot Tomlinson was pulling him out of the car.

"Is he dead, Henry?" the gruff voice asked.

"Nah. He's groaning and carryin' on. I think I got him in the head or neck. He leaned forward just as I shot or he would be dead."

"All right, you drive. See if the key is in the ignition."

The man named Henry fumbled around and found the ignition switch. He started the engine and said, "Now what?"

"See if you can drive out of here without turning on the headlights. I'll keep this bitch cop quiet. I think we'll just keep her as our hostage. Maybe we can get something out of her. Anyhow, when you get out on the road, turn on the lights and start driving toward town—fast. We may have to fight our way out of here, so be ready for that."

Mary Ellen sat crammed between the two men. Her head was spinning from being manhandled by her captor, who sat with one arm wrapped around her neck and his pistol jammed in her ribs. Her only thought was to find some way to get to the pistol in the glove compartment. The man named Henry managed to get the car to the main road after going over many bushes and ramming into several trees in the dark. While he was doing it, a voice came on the radio saying: "Control, what is your status?" Mary Ellen knew it was Marcus.

"Answer it," the gruff voice commanded, pressing the gun barrel harder against Mary Ellen's ribs.

"What should I say?"

"Say everything is fine."

Mary Ellen keyed the microphone. "Everything is fine . . . Howard."

Once on the main road, Henry revved the engine, turned on the lights, and pushed the accelerator to the floor.

Marcus and Deputy Hank Cronnin had heard the single shot coming from the direction of the control car. When Mary Ellen called him Howard on the radio, he knew something was wrong. He was relieved to hear Mary Ellen's voice, but he knew he had to act fast. He told Cronnin to start their car and move to the main road, but just as they were about to pull onto it, the control car whizzed past them. In their headlights, they could see a stranger driving.

As Cronnin wheeled into the chase, Marcus got on the radio and called for all three other cars to converge on the main road headed for town. Cronnin was an expert driver, having chased quite a few bootleggers in the past. He kept up with the fleeing car, but none of the other cars were in position to join in the chase.

"Stay with him, Hank," Marcus ordered. "But don't get too close."

In the car ahead, Mary Ellen could see the speedometer needle pointing to 75 miles per hour. The car careened badly from side to side over the rough road. Gruff Voice turned in his seat and began firing with his pistol with his left hand at the pursuing squad car. When he did, Mary Ellen tried to move forward toward the glove compartment, but Gruff Voice felt her move. He slammed her in the head with his left elbow, throwing her over onto Henry as he drove and causing the car to swerve badly. After a frightening moment, Henry regained control of the car and shoved Mary Ellen's limp body away.

In his car, Marcus had seen the red flashes of gun shots coming from the car ahead. He heard one bullet hit somewhere on the body of his car, and immediately he felt the concussion from another that tore through the roof over his head.

"I can't fire back." Marcus said. "Mary Ellen and Tomlinson are probably in that car."

"At these speeds, this won't last long," said Cronnin. "He nearly lost it just then. One wrong move and he's going to lose control."

Cronnin was right. The car ahead went into a sharp turn way too fast. Its rear end swung out and its wheels left the ground. Cronnin got his car slowed enough to watch as the other car rolled over three times and came to rest in a corn field. As the car tumbled, the doors broke opened and all three passengers went flying out. The car rolled over Henry, crushing him to death. Mary Ellen and Gruff Voice landed in the corn field as the car rolled on past. Marcus leapt out of his car before it fully stopped and, with his revolver drawn, ran crashing through the rows of corn to the scene. The car lay upside down with its wheels spinning in the air. Hissing sounds came from the ruptured radiator, and the smell of gasoline was strong. Marcus found Mary

Ellen a few yards away lying face down in crushed corn stalks. "Oh my God!" he muttered.

He gently turned her over and brushed the dirt from her face. Her body was limp. She did not seem to be breathing. Marcus placed the side of his head on her breast to listen for a heartbeat. There was one! Faint, but definitely there. He felt her arms and legs—no signs of broken bones, and no blood. This was good. Maybe she was going to be OK.

At the same time, Cronnin, also with gun in hand, examined the dead driver and went to stand over the other man, who was unconscious. The way his body was twisted, he appeared to have a broken back. Within minutes, the other three cars arrived and the six officers went to work. They set up road blocks on both sides of the scene, and Sheriff Braxton told them to search anyone who showed up and arrest any who were armed. "There are probably more of them," he told the deputies. Then he got on his radio and called for the ambulance from Williams Funeral Home, the only ambulance in the county.

When Braxton came to talk with him, Marcus was still holding Mary Ellen. "What about her? Has she said anything?" Braxton asked.

"Still out of it, but I think she is going to come around. She's breathing easier and her eyes fluttered a moment ago."

Mary Ellen's eyes came open, but could not focus. She reached with one hand for Marcus' face. "Is that you, Marcus?" she whispered.

"It's me, Mary Ellen. Do you hurt anywhere?"

"Yes."

"Where?"

"All over."

"Can you move your hands and feet?"

"Yes, but I don't want to."

Marcus looked up at Braxton. "I think we got lucky."

Mary Ellen moaned but managed to say, "They shot Agent Tomlinson."

"Where?"

"Back where we were. They threw him in the woods."

Braxton motioned to one of his deputies and told him to take his car back to where the control car had been stationed to look for Tomlinson. "Take your partner with you, and be damned careful. There's bound to be more of this gang around here somewhere. Also, be on the lookout for Sgt. Bailey. He's out in those woods. He'll probably come to you when he sees the lights."

It was almost half an hour before the ambulance arrived. The two attendants were not medically trained, but they were experienced. They laid a blanket beside the injured man and as gently as possible, worked it under him. Then, with the help of two deputies, they lifted the blanket and eased him onto the stretcher. He groaned constantly, and cried out several times. When they came to get Mary Ellen, they used the same procedure. She was obviously not hurt as badly as the other man, but she might have internal injuries. Marcus was not happy about Mary Ellen being put in the same ambulance with one of the attackers. He told his deputy, Wilford Simpson, to ride in the ambulance and keep an eye on him. He would come to the hospital to see about Mary Ellen as soon as he could.

The two deputies Sheriff Braxton had sent to find Tomlinson were not sure where to look, and when Marcus got to the area they had found nothing yet. Marcus knew exactly where the control car had been hidden and he drove to it, followed by the two deputies. They searched around with flashlights and found the FBI agent unconscious and lying face down on the blood-soaked ground. The bullet had cut a gash along the base of his skull, taking off the lobe of his ear, which hung down from a strip of skin. Blood was still oozing out of the wound, so Marcus broke out the first aid kit in his car, bandaged it, and then pressed on it firmly with the palm of his hand to stop the bleeding. Tomlinson was in shock, so Marcus carried him to the squad car and placed him in the back seat where he covered him with a blanket.

About then, Sgt. Bailey appeared and got the full story from one of the deputies. He then reported to Marcus. "Did anyone come to pick up the package in the mailbox?" Marcus asked.

"Not in a car, but I think someone did it on foot. I heard something. I tried to contact the control car on my radio, but there was no answer."

"Could you tell how many of them there were?"

"No. It was too dark."

Marcus instructed the two deputies to check the mailbox to see if anything was in it and then proceed to town. There, he headed straight for the hospital. When he got there, he helped hospital orderlies get Agent Tomlinson out of the back seat and take him to the emergency room.

The doctor on duty was Howard Green, a white haired physician of the old school who had seen car wreck injuries before. He examined the injured man first, with Deputy Simpson watching everything. Dr. Green had the injured man put in mild traction, sutured three cuts, and gave him morphine for the pain. He then looked at Mary Ellen and determined that although she would be too sore and banged up to get out of bed for several days, she had no major injuries. He gave her something to sleep and an analgesic for the pain and soreness. "Thank God she landed in a plowed field and the car did not roll over on her," he told Marcus when he got to the hospital.

Agent Tomlinson had come out of shock on the trip to the hospital. Dr. Green cleansed and disinfected his wound and sewed it up neatly. He even sewed back the lobe of Tomlinson's ear. "He lost a lot of blood, and he's going to have an ugly scar, but the bullet took away very little bone mass, and there was no damage to the brain. He'll be all right. And down the road, a plastic surgeon may be able to do something about the scar," he told Marcus. "Who shot him?"

"The other fellow you worked on," Marcus answered. "He's facing charges of attempted murder and a lot of other things. There's also one that was killed in the crash. The deputies took him to the funeral home."

"You folks lead exciting lives, don't you?" Dr. Green observed.

"Exciting!" Marcus looked into the room where Mary Ellen was sleeping. "I'm sorry I ever heard that word."

# CHAPTER 11

Ruth Selvedge sat beside Marcus as they drove from Franklin to the hospital in Marion early the next morning. With the same blond hair, perfect skin, and blue eyes, she was almost as beautiful as Mary Ellen and only twenty years older. But it was anything but a comfortable trip. Ruth was so angry at Marcus that she would not speak. His assurances that Mary Ellen was not badly hurt brought nothing from her but stony silence.

At the hospital, Mary Ellen was sitting up in bed when her mother entered. "Mother! What are you doing here? Who's running the café?" were her first words.

"I'm here to find out about you. I closed the café."

"Oh."

"Are you all right, dear? Marcus says you were captured and then in a car wreck and that a man was shot sitting next to you. For heaven's sake! What have you gotten into?"

"I'm all right, Mother. A few scrapes and bruises. They are just keeping me here for observation. Dr. Green says I can leave tomorrow."

Ruth sighed in mixture of relief and disapproval. "I just can't believe all of this is happening!"

Mary Ellen looked past her mother to Marcus. "What about Agent Tomlinson? Is he dead?"

"No, the bullet grazed his head and ear. Dr. Green sewed him up, and he is going to be all right."

"Oh, thank God! I was so worried. And what about the two men that attacked us?"

"One is dead—the one who was driving. The other one—his name is Carney—has a broken back. He is here in the hospital, but he will be arrested as soon as he can be moved."

"So where does all of this leave us?" Mary Ellen asked. "We still don't know where Amanda is or whether the bunch we were dealing with really has her."

"Mary Ellen!" Ruth exclaimed, "You are *not* still playing detective!"

Mary Ellen managed a weak smile. "I'm afraid so, Mother."

"Well, I'll be damned," Ruth muttered. She did not swear often, but the situation seemed to warrant it.

This time, Marcus smiled. "Mrs. Selvedge, we are going to stay on the case, but I promise that in the future we will do everything we can to avoid situations like last night."

He turned to Mary Ellen. "I figure there's more of the gang. The deputies are out looking for a car left in that area. It they don't find one, it would indicate there are more of them and they let those two assassins out of a car so they could sneak up on you. Also, someone picked up the package in the mailbox last night. He was probably on foot. Since the two men that attacked you did not have the package on them, there has to be more of the gang." Marcus was reasoning as he talked.

"Maybe I can leave here today," Mary Ellen said as she attempted to swing her legs to the floor. It caused her to moan in pain and fall back on her pillow. "Dr. Green warned me I would be sore," she said between clenched teeth. "He was sure as heck right."

Marcus nodded. "OK, you take it easy today. I'll come back over here tomorrow morning to take you home." He turned back to Ruth. "Mrs. Selvedge, I'm going to the Court House to talk with Sheriff Braxton. I'll come back to get you in an hour or so." He left quickly, happy to escape Ruth's hostile glare.

Sheriff Braxton was in his office in the Williamson County Court House. "How's that pretty detective of yours?" he asked.

"She's so sore she can't get out of bed, but the doctor says she is going to be all right."

"I got a report on Agent Tomlinson. He's lucky to be alive. A few inches to the left and that bullet would have killed or paralyzed him."

"Yes, very lucky. What do you know about the two men that attacked us? Are they from around here?"

"They are. Both of them hang out at the Shady Rest. The dead one is Henry Pfister. He has done time in Joliet for robbery and assault. The other fellow is Roy Carney, a part-time coal miner and full time trouble-maker. I've had to pick him up three or four times for drunk and disorderly. He likes to hurt people."

"Are they members of a gang?"

"Probably, but I don't know who's the leader or who else is in it."

"The main thing now is to find out if this gang is holding Amanda Newcombe, and if they are, where? Do you have any ideas about that?"

Braxton shook his head. "It could be any one of a hundred different places in this county or in the next one. What we need to know is who these people are. That might lead us to their hideout, which may be where the woman is being held."

"You think the gang is connected to the Shady Rest?"

"I'd bet on it, but it would be a tough job to find out for sure."

"We need an informant—someone on the inside."

"Now that would be a dangerous occupation. Those characters out at the Shady Rest would cut an informant up into little pieces if they caught him."

"Yeah, I guess you are right." Marcus liked Braxton, but he could see there was a limit to what he was willing to do about the Shady Rest. "I'll head back to Jefferson County and go talk with Mr. Newcombe. If this gang does have his wife, they will get in touch with him again. I'll just have to work this case from that end."

"Tell you what I will do, Marcus. I'll tell my deputies to keep an eye on the Shady Rest and I'll have my detective nose around and see what he can find out about some sort of gang out there. If we turn up anything, I'll let you know right away. "

"That will be fine. I'll call you if Newcombe hears from the gang again." Marcus left after thanking Braxton for his department's good work the night before.

On the way back to Franklin, Marcus and Ruth had a frank talk about Mary Ellen's career as a detective. Ruth had tried without success for almost an hour to persuade Mary Ellen to give it up. Finally, she was resigned to the idea of her daughter as a crime fighter. She was not happy about it, but Mary Ellen was no child. She could decide for herself.

Ruth suspected there was more to the situation than either Mary Ellen or Marcus were admitting. One look at Marcus sitting next to her in the squad car was enough to give her the idea there might be another reason for Mary Ellen wanting to be a detective. Marcus was definitely a fine looking man. He had the kind of looks that turned heads, both men's and women's, when he walked into a room. But it wasn't just looks. He had an air of confidence and easiness that made you want to get to know him better. He certainly was not a typical sheriff, but neither did he seem out of place in the job. His slow, unruffled manner, Ruth imagined, could change to quick action when needed. Strength— carefully controlled strength—that was what described him. Yes, she could see how Mary Ellen, who had turned down so many men, might finally be attracted to Marcus Dixon.

The two talked until they reached an understanding. Ruth would accept that Mary Ellen was going to be a part-time detective and Marcus would do everything he could to see that nothing terrible happened to her on the job. In fact, Marcus spoke with such conviction about how he would protect Mary Ellen that Ruth sensed much more than professional interest.

Later that day, Marcus went to Zeigler to talk with Richard Newcombe. He told him what had happened the night before in Williamson County. "Then we still don't know if these are the people who have Amanda?" Newcombe asked.

"That's right. If they are the ones, you will hear from them again soon. If not, I think we can assume they were phonies and start looking for her elsewhere. In fact, I am going to do that anyhow. I've decided to send someone to Chicago to look into Amanda's family and friends. I will need names and addresses from you—your father-in-law and any of Amanda's friends that live in the Chicago area."

"Certainly, but why do you have to bother Mr. Littleton? He's a very busy man."

"I doubt if he's too busy to help find his missing daughter," Marcus answered.

When Marcus got back to his office, there were two FBI agents waiting for him. Their names were Sanford Wells and Alex Ruud. Both looked somewhat like their predecessor Tomlinson—dark suits, clean shaven, slight balding and a no nonsense attitude.

Wells seemed to be the agent in charge. He wanted a full report from Marcus on what had happened. He already knew about Agent Tomlinson being shot, having talked with him on the phone. "We take a dim view of our agents getting shot from behind," he commented when Marcus had finished. "We are going after this gang that seems to be operating out of the Shady Rest, and we would appreciate your full cooperation."

"That gang took my detective captive and nearly got her killed. I'm going after them too." Marcus said grimly.

Two days passed, and Mary Ellen came back to work at the café. Marcus had lunch there and inquired how she was feeling. She looked fine, except for a scratch on her forehead and a lack of ease in her movements. She said she was well, but Marcus was concerned. Back at his office, Sgt. Bailey asked if Mary Ellen was coming in that day.

"I don't know, Orville. She's over at the café working today. She says she's OK."

"She may have had enough of being a detective, you know. I wouldn't blame her," Bailey observed.

"Maybe," said Marcus. "But she's made of pretty good stuff."

Soon after the regular closing time, Mary Ellen marched into the sheriff's office, dressed in an attractive gray suit and wearing her badge. "Ready for duty," she told Marcus and Bailey.

Marcus winked at Bailey and motioned for her to have a seat. "I'll fill you in on what's been happening. First of all, the FBI has sent two agents this time. They are going to try to run down the gang that we think is operating out of the Shady Rest. They are down in Williamson County now working on that. Sheriff Braxton called me this morning and reported that the FBI doesn't seem to be making much progress. They questioned Roy Carney in the hospital but got nowhere. He's in a lot of pain, but even if he wasn't, he probably wouldn't talk much. Second, Newcombe has heard nothing from the supposed kidnappers. I talked with him this morning on the phone"

"What do you make of that?" Mary Ellen asked.

"I'm beginning to have serious doubts that the gang from Shady Rest really has Amanda. I think she may be somewhere else."

"So what do we do next?" asked Bailey.

"As I have said all along, we are going to have to take a closer look at Newcombe. That means someone needs to go to Chicago and interview Amanda's family and friends. That's where this case seems to be leading."

"I'll go," said Mary Ellen quickly.

"By yourself?" Bailey wanted to know.

"Yes, by myself."

"Well, I can't go to Chicago," Marcus added. "I have to be here. I'll be working on the Newcombe case, but it's not the only thing I have to deal with here in the county. I can't leave for five or six days, or whatever it would take."

"Then what about it?" Mary Ellen asked. "Do you want me to go?"

Marcus thought for a minute. He had come to admire Mary Ellen's spunk. She probably could handle herself in the big city. He would provide the names she needed to get started—Randolph Littleton and Chief Kelly, and she could check on Hanley Friedman's old haunts. He couldn't afford to send two people to Chicago and weaken his small force, so sending Mary Ellen made sense. Besides, the novelty of a beautiful detective might prove to be productive. At least people, and especially men, would pay attention to her.

"OK. You are going. I guess you will get your mother to run the café."

Mary Ellen nodded. Marcus did not intend to frequent the City Café while Mary Ellen was gone. He knew Ruth Selvedge would be more than he wanted to deal with.

# CHAPTER 12

Marcus drove Mary Ellen to catch the *City of New Orleans* at the station in DuQuoin. The train was due there at 3:13 a.m. and would make only a brief stop. Driving down the lonely two-lane highway, the two sat silently, lost in personal thoughts. Mary Ellen was excited and—although she would never admit it—scared. She had never been to Chicago. In fact, she had never been out of Southern Illinois. Sure, she had seen movies about Chicago—mostly gangster pictures with tough guys like Jimmy Cagney and George Raft throwing bombs into store fronts and wiping out other gangs with Tommy guns. The most famous man in Chicago was Al Capone, and the city had a reputation for being a rough place. What would it be like there? Would people be friendly and helpful like most people in Southern Illinois? She had heard that Chicagoans looked on everyone downstate as hicks. They wouldn't even give you the time of day—that was the expression.

Mary Ellen thought about Nora Charles. Nora didn't go off doing detective work on her own. Nick was always there. But her Nick—Marcus—was not going to be with her in Chicago. There was no denying she wanted Marcus to be there. She wanted that a lot. But she was going alone. The people she would have to deal with would be mostly men. Mary Ellen knew the effect her looks had on men—the widening of their eyes, the stare and the look up and down. Usually, she handled that situation simply by being formal but not unfriendly.

One ugly name that was almost never applied to Mary Ellen was prick teaser. She just wasn't that.

Mary Ellen knew she was beautiful, but she did not try to enhance it with make-up, jewelry, or overly stylish clothes. She had a style of her own. She dressed simply, wore little jewelry, and never tinted her hair. Her approach with men was to accept their interest, but to do it on a one-human-to-another basis rather than a sexual one. But would that work in Chicago where people were likely to be different?

Marcus was thinking similar thoughts. He knew Mary Ellen was a small town girl, maybe a bit naïve. Was he putting her in real danger by sending her to Chicago? Marcus had been to the city several times during his football days and had visited friends there. He knew that everyone in Chicago was not a gangster. All kinds of people lived there, but that was the problem—some of the people in Chicago were definitely bad. What if Mary Ellen got in the hands of one of them? Would she be streetwise enough to avoid dangerous situations? True, she was not going to Chicago to arrest anyone, just to interview people, but what about cab drivers, hotel clerks, men in restaurants, and men who saw her on the street? Would she be able to handle all those situations?

When they turned into the parking lot and stopped, Marcus turned to Mary Elllen and put his hand on her shoulder. She looked at him in surprise.

"You have never been to Chicago, have you?" he said.

"No."

"Then maybe we ought not to do this."

"Do what?"

"Go to Chicago."

"But you are not going."

"That's just it. You are going alone."

She put her hand on his chest. "Are you worried about me?"

"Yes. I promised your mother . . ."

"I know, but what are you worried about?"

"You know what. You are so damned beautiful that men get ideas when they are around you."

"Well, thanks—I guess."

"I'm serious. It's a problem sometimes, isn't it? And it will be a lot worse when you are in a city full of strangers."

"I'll be careful."

Marcus put his arms around her and pulled her to him. For an instant, she resisted in surprise, but then she softened against him and lifted her face. Her eyes glowed in the dim light from the dashboard. He kissed her, and she moaned softly as her arms went around his neck. Marcus held her close. "I couldn't handle it if something happened to you," he whispered in her hair.

The kiss had changed everything. Mary Ellen's mind went blank. She had no idea of what to say or do next. She had never been kissed like that before. It was not a seductive kiss or one burning with passion, but it reached into her soul and made her feel loved. Mary Ellen's only thought was that she would remember this moment for the rest of her life.

The whistle of the approaching train broke the silence of the night. Marcus opened the car door and said, "We've got to get you a ticket." They got out of the car and walked to the station with Marcus carrying her bag. Neither spoke. There would be much to talk about later.

Marcus stood unhappily on the platform and looked at Mary Ellen sitting in the darkened chair car as the *City of New Orleans* pulled from the station. He hardly heard the thundering and hissing of the big steam locomotive. He was worried about Mary Ellen going off to Chicago alone. But it was done now.

When Marcus got to the court house Mrs. Fallon was already in the jail kitchen rattling pots and pans preparing for breakfast. He told her he would want breakfast and went to check his office. Sgt. Bailey had left a note on his desk that read, "Alfred Zalesky over in Zeigler may have some information." Marcus folded the note slowly, put it in his shirt pocket, and then went to breakfast. *This*, he told himself, *could be something*.

It was mid-morning when Marcus' Chevy drove into Zeigler. It was probably too early, Marcus thought, to find Alfred Zalesky at Hunker's Place, although there would likely be a few beer drinkers there already. Maureen would be at work, and Zalesky might be at home, or maybe working in the mine today. Marcus saw a middle aged woman walking down the street carrying a bag of groceries. He pulled over to the curb and leaned out of his window.

"Mornin' Ma'am," he said. "What did they blow this morning?"

"Morning," the woman said, a bit wary as she eyed the sheriff's seal on the door of the coupe. "They blew one."

"Much obliged." Marcus pinched the brim of his grey felt hat and drove on. He knew now that the mine whistle had signaled that the mine was working today. Al Zalesky would either be working or drinking at Hunker's Place. Not all miners would start drinking so early, but Zalesky was one who would.

He was right. Only a handful of patrons occupied Hunker's, but Zalesky was one of them. Marcus walked to the table where he was sitting with several other men. "Let's have a little talk, Al," he said coolly, nodding toward another table.

Zalesky stood and walked to the table, carrying his beer mug.

"I'm told you may have some information for me," Marcus began.

Zalesky took a small sip of beer. "Could be. You haven't found Newcombe's wife yet, have you?"

"No, we haven't."

"Well, I've been hearing some stuff that might mean she was not kidnapped."

"Hearing? What does that mean?"

"It's just sort of rumors. But some people believe that Newcombe may have something to do with her disappearance."

"Look, I didn't drive over here to listen to a bunch of vague rumors. Have you got something to tell me, or not?"

"Yeah, I have got an eye witness."

Marcus was getting annoyed. "Witness to what?"

"Amos Freeling, this old codger that lives on the road that goes around behind Number 3 Mine, he says he saw Newcombe's big Packard parked up there on the road near his house one night about a week ago. It was about the time Newcombe's wife disappeared."

"How did he know it was Newcombe?"

"I guess it was because he said it was a big, late model sedan—Newcombe has the only one in town."

"So, what is suspicious about it being parked there?"

"What the hell was he doing up there at night? That's what's suspicious. And also, the place where it was parked is close to an old mine air shaft. It would be a great place to throw a body."

"Why?"

"That section of the mine is closed—walled off. You can't get in there."

"Well, isn't the old air shaft covered?'

"Sure, but it's covered with a plank deck that can be lifted off. Like I said, it's a great place to throw a body."

"Did this old codger see anything like a body being thrown in there?"

"You'll have to ask him."

Marcus looked steadily at Zalesky who turned away and took another drink of beer.

"You don't like Newcombe very much, do you?" he asked.

"Nobody around here likes him—damned fancy pants manager from Chicago. Married the boss's daughter. He's about the most *disliked* son of a bitch in town."

"Why is that?"

"Oh, hell. It's just the way he acts—always acting like a big shot, thinks he's better than us coal miners. I'll bet you that piss ant has never been down in a mine since he got here. Might get his fancy clothes dirty. I'd like to see one of his white shirts after he's been down in a mine. It might start a new style—charcoal colored shirts."

"OK. I get the picture. Any other reason you don't like him?" Marcus thought about adding *"Other than the fact that he is sleeping with your wife?"*

Zalesky looked at him sharply. "What are you getting at?"

"Nothing. Have you got anything else?"

"No. Ain't what I told you enough?"

"We'll see. If you have anything else, let me know." Marcus stood and without further pleasantries, turned and walked out. Zalesky watched him leave, wondered what effect his story would have.

Marcus drove to the Number 3 Mine and took the road that led up the gentle hill behind the mine entry. As he passed the tipple, he could see the conveyor was raising newly mined coal out of the mine and dumping it onto a waiting truck. The mine was definitely working today. He wondered why Al Zalesky had not gone to work. Obviously, he seemed to have had other business to take care of.

The house of Amos Freeling—it was more like a shack—sat next to the road behind the mine. Marcus knocked on the front door, and soon a grizzled old man in dirty overalls peered through a tattered screen door that would have admitted a squadron of flies.

"Whaddaya want?" he growled.

"Freeling, I'm the Sheriff. I want to ask you some questions."

"I know who you are. Whaddaya want to ask?"

"Is it true that you saw a big car parked on the road near the old air shaft one night last week?"

"Yeah, it's true."

"What night was it?"

"I dunno. Monday or Tuesday."

"What time?"

"About one o'clock. I got up because the dogs was barkin'." Marcus had not noticed until then that two coon dogs were sleeping next to the porch.

"How long did the car stay?"

"Dunno. I went back to bed."

"Could you tell how many were in the car?"

"Nah. Too dark."

"How about showing me where the car was parked."

"Hell, I'm fixin my meal, Sheriff."

"Look, Freeling, do you want to cooperate here or not?"

"All right, all right. Let me get my hat."

In a moment, the screen door swung open, Freeling came out, and the two coon dogs stretched and got to their feet. Freeling led Marcus to a spot about 80 yards from his shack. He pointed to a wide place in the road and indicated it was where the car had been parked. Marcus squatted and looked for tire tracks. There was one set where a car had obviously pulled off the road. The tracks were distinct, deeply cut with sharp edges indicating fairly new tires. They had a pattern of alternating squares and chevrons. Marcus looked around further but found nothing that might have been thrown out of the car—no cigarette butts, no tissues, no used condoms.

"Now, show me the old air shaft," Marcus said. Freeling pointed to a wooden platform partially hidden by weeds only about twenty yards up the hill. Marcus walked to it carefully, looking for footprints or trampled weeds and finding none. The platform had once been painted but now badly needed maintenance. Marcus examined it carefully, but could find no sign that it had recently been raised. He slipped his fingers under the 1 by 12 board that framed the platform and began to lift.

"I'd be careful there Sheriff," Freeling said, backing away. "That old mine was pretty gassy."

Marcus lifted the platform enough to clear it off the ground and waited. There was a good breeze, and after a few minutes he figured it was safe to raise it high enough to look underneath. What he saw was a hole in the ground about five feet across. No doubt about it, this was a fine place to dispose of a dead body. The shaft probably went down several hundred feet. Only a very strong light would be able to shine down in there, and then you probably couldn't see the bottom.  For anyone to go down into the shaft on a rope or cable would be doubly dangerous because of the depth and the strong possibility of methane gas.

Marcus put the platform back in place, dusted his hands, and thanked Freeling for his help. As he drove back to town, he decided he definitely needed to know if there was a body at the bottom of the shaft. His next step, then, was to talk with the mine manager about opening the walled off section of the mine.  But guess who the mine manager was—Newcombe, the same person who may have thrown a body down the shaft. Marcus reasoned that Newcombe's reaction to the idea of opening the abandoned section of the mine would be very revealing. His next step was to propose it to Newcombe.

Maureen Zalesky gave Marcus her usual warm greeting when he walked into the Consolidated Coal office. "Well," she smiled, "look who's here again." She pushed back from her desk so Marcus could see the tight fitting new dress she was wearing.

"Hello, Maureen. I need to see Newcombe."

Marcus looked at the dress appreciatively. He had always liked Maureen. There was no meanness in her—just a woman who liked men and appreciated having a good time. He would have difficulty believing she had anything to do with Amanda's disappearance. It was true she was playing around with her boss, but Marcus doubted if it was more than just that, especially on Newcombe's part. He was too crafty and ambitious to get involved in any kind of permanent arrangement with someone like Maureen.

Maureen waved toward Newcombe's office. "Sure, go on in,"

As usual, Newcombe was the picture of the up-and-coming young executive—well shaved and combed and wearing a tailored brown suit and silk tie. His desk was clear, except for a two-pen desk set and the folder he was reading.

"Anything new Sheriff," he asked.

"Yes, but first, have you heard any more from the supposed kidnappers?"

"Not a word."

"Then I'll tell you why I am here. We have had a report that a large, late model sedan was seen parked up behind Number 3 Mine one night last week, parked near the closed air shaft of that part of the mine." Marcus watched Newcombe carefully while he said this.

Newcombe slowly closed the folder he was reading and, without looking up, said, "I don't understand. What has that got to do with anything?"

"The suggestion has been made that maybe someone threw a body down that old air shaft, someone driving a large, late model sedan."

Newcombe looked up, his eyes blazing. "Someone has suggested! Oh! I get it. One of these redneck miners is trying to say I killed my wife. I have a late model sedan. I guess that proves it. Son of a bitch! There are plenty of vicious people in this rotten little town, and they would like nothing better than to pin something like that on me."

"Relax," said Marcus. "You're jumping to conclusions. The reason I'm here is to talk with you about going into that part of the mine to see if there is a body at the bottom of the shaft."

"You mean you believe this pile of crap?"

"It's a legitimate lead. I have to investigate it."

"Investigate it. What does that mean?"

"What I said. Send someone into that part of the mine."

"Hell, man. You don't know what you are asking. That part of the mine has been abandoned and walled off for years. We can't just open it up. It might release methane gas throughout the mine. And I can't send anyone in there searching. It could mean their death."

Marcus noted that all of this reasoning was nicely convenient if indeed Newcombe had thrown Amanda's body down the shaft.

"What about the mine rescue team? They have breathing apparatuses, and they are trained in this sort of thing."

Newcombe thought for a moment. "I suppose we could try that. It's a state team. I'd have to go to the state mine safety people."

"You could use my name. It might help if they know it's part of a crime investigation," Marcus offered.

"But good Lord! I would have to shut down the mine—take everyone out while they were doing it. And even at that, there's danger of an explosion. They sure won't like it at company headquarters."

"Maybe if they know why we're doing it, they will like it better—especially Mr. Littleton, since we are trying to find his daughter."

"You don't know him very well."

When Marcus got back to his office, his sergeant, Orville Bailey asked what he had learned from Al Zalesky.

"Quite a bit. He told me about a fellow who might have seen someone throw a body down the old air shaft of Number 3 Mine. He also said that lots of people in Zeigler suspect that Newcombe had something to do with his wife's disappearance."

"Did you believe him?"

"Enough to check out his story about the air shaft."

"What about Newcombe?"

"Well, one thing's for sure. Al Zalesky has no use for Newcombe. He was obviously trying to get him in trouble. My guess is that he knows that Newcombe is sleeping with his wife, and he is trying to get even with him."

"You think Newcombe might have killed his wife?"

"Might have—yes. His whole attitude from the beginning has made me suspicious. And then, there is the complete lack of real clues in this case. It's as if someone had made a great effort to make Amanda disappear without a trace. And who would be in a better position to do that than Newcombe?"

"But if he killed her, why would he throw her body down the air shaft of his own mine?"

"Think about it. Is there a better place anywhere around here to get rid of a body? It's perfect. That part of the mine is sealed off and can't be entered. And what's more, who do you think would know that? And who is actually in control of everything that happens in Number 3 Mine?"

Bailey smiled wryly and shook his head. The questions did not need answers.

# CHAPTER 13

The skyscrapers and bustle of Chicago did not overwhelm Mary Ellen as she rode in a taxi to her hotel. But the crowded streets excited her, and her pounding heart told her she was a bit frightened. The Bismark Hotel, a recommendation from Marcus, proved to be a somber affair with a large tile-floored lobby strewn with leather chairs. Stained glass signs proclaimed easy access to a dining room and bar. The desk clerk, a well-dressed young man with slicked-back hair, looked her over critically and finally found the reservation Marcus had made by telegraph.

"Yes, here we have it, Miss . . . hm Selvedge. A room for one. The reservation was made by a Sheriff Dixon, so you will be getting the professional discount. We have quite a few police officers staying here, but I must say that none of the others are as charming as you."

Mary Ellen did not react. "May I have my key, please?"

"Yes, of course." The clerk handed her the key and rang for a bellhop. A young fellow in a uniform quickly appeared and picked up Mary Ellen's bag. "This way, Miss," he said with a forced smile. In the elevator, he tried to make conversation, but Mary Ellen stuck to polite yes and no answers.

The hotel room was small and simply furnished. The bellhop opened the only window, which had a view of another tall building and the street below. Then he worked the lever to open the transom over the door. "You're gonna need some air in here tonight," he said. "Want me to turn on the ceiling fan?"

Mary Ellen nodded yes and tipped him a dollar for such considerate service. There was an awkward moment when the bellboy stood smiling but did not leave.

"Can I get anything for you Miss? Maybe some ice or something to drink?"

"No, nothing, thank you." When Mary Ellen placed her hand on the door knob as if to close it, the bellboy got the message and left. As she unpacked, Mary Ellen went over her plan in her mind. The first step was to get in touch with Chief Kelly of the Consolidation Coal Company police and work through him to arrange interviews with all of Amanda's family. She found a number for Consolidation Coal in the unbelievably thick phone book and called. The operator put her through to Chief Kelly, who was surprised to hear from a female detective from the Sheriff's Department in Jefferson County but willing to cooperate. He told Mary Ellen how to get to his office, and they made an appointment for the next morning.

Mary Ellen had dinner in the hotel dining room and went back to her room, where she had a detective novel to read. About 9:30 the friendly bellhop knocked on her door and asked if there was anything she needed, but she did not let him in the room and told him pleasantly that she was quite comfortable. Soon after, the desk clerk called her room to ask if there was anything he could do to make her stay more pleasant. She thanked him for the offer but declined.

Next morning, Mary Ellen had breakfast in the dining room, not without observing to herself what a luxury it was to have someone else prepare and serve her breakfast.

The cab trip to Consolidation Coal's building in the morning traffic took a good thirty minutes, although it was only a few miles. Mary Ellen marveled at how people could deal with such delays and frustrations on a daily basis.

Consolidation Coal occupied a five story building on the south side of Chicago. The office of the company police was on the first floor. A receptionist in the lobby guided Mary Ellen to the office, which looked more like a business office than a police station. A secretary showed Mary Ellen into Chief Kelly's office. With a name like Kelly,

Mary Ellen expected to see an Irishman, and she was not disappointed. Mike Kelly could have acted in movies as an Irish beat cop. With his round, smiling face and reddish hair, he reminded Mary Ellen of the actor Pat O'Brian, only slightly older.

"Well, well," he said warmly as he shook Mary Ellen's hand. "A lady sheriff's detective, is it? And a pretty one at that."

Mary Ellen accepted the familiarity easily. "That's right, Chief. And how about you? An Irish policeman in Chicago. I've heard there are a few of them."

Kelly's hearty laugh caused the departing secretary to look back at him.

"OK, Detective Selvedge, we're even. What can I do for you?"

Mary Ellen filled him in on the recent events in the Amanda Newcombe case, including the lack of any further communication from the supposed kidnappers. "We suspect now that the people we were dealing with do not have Amanda. The FBI is working on it, but I am here in Chicago to look into the possibility that she may not have been kidnapped at all. She may have left on her own and is in hiding somewhere."

"Why would you think that?" Kelly asked.

"There is no real evidence that she was kidnapped or murdered. She is simply missing, which raises the possibility I mentioned."

"So what do you want to do here in Chicago?"

"Talk with the family and any close friends about her state of mind."

"I suppose you want to start with Mr. Littleton."

"Yes, and could you help me locate the rest of the family?"

"Sure, that won't be difficult. There are only two other family members, her mother and her sister. The sister has a husband and two children. I'll give you their addresses and phone numbers. As for seeing Mr. Littleton, I'll try to set up something this afternoon."

Mary Ellen waited while Kelly talked on the intercom. "OK. You can see him at 2:30. His office is on the top floor. Anything else I can do for you?"

"Well, Sheriff Dixon has briefed me on what he learned from you earlier, how you and your officers watched Amanda during the time when she had a romance with Hanley Friedman. Is there anything else you can tell me about that?"

"Let me think. . . I'd have to say that those two were very close. I don't know for sure whether they ever slept together or not—some things you can't determine watching from a distance, you know. But they never went to a hotel together while we were watching them."

"What makes you think they were so close?"

"Oh, time spent together, body language—that sort of thing. She really seemed to fall into a funk when they broke up. She didn't go out of the house for days on end, and when she did, she just walked the streets, looking pretty sad."

"How long did you watch her after they broke up?"

"Until her engagement to Newcombe was announced."

"What do you think of Newcombe?"

"The boss likes him. He's efficient and as far as I know honest, at least with company matters."

"Not honest in other matters?"

"Maybe. He had a reputation as a ladies' man, and it continued after he was married. But now I'm giving you gossip. I have no evidence."

"What about Hanley Friedman? Did you investigate him?"

"Sure. He comes from a good Jewish family that lives on the Near North Side. The father is in the clothing business. He's a buyer for Sears and Roebuck. They're not rich, but certainly not poor. Hanley went to Northwestern. That's where he met Amanda—in an English literature class. He's pretty artsy—writes poetry and tries to look like a poet."

"Yes, I've met him. Has he ever been in trouble with the police?"

Kelly laughed. "Nope. We checked on that."

"What did he do after they broke up?"

"Got a job teaching in the CCC. I told your sheriff about it."

Mary Ellen got addresses and phone numbers from Kelly and went to lunch at a nearby café that the Chief recommended. Then she came to the lobby of Consolidated Coal building and sat until time for her appointment with Littleton. She used the time to write notes on her conversation with Chief Kelly.

At 2:15, she took the elevator to the top floor and found the office of the president. A rather plain, older woman sat in the outer office behind an uncluttered desk, flanked by rows of file cabinets. She looked to be the model of efficiency as well as a strict gatekeeper for her boss. She eyed Mary Ellen suspiciously and showed her into a large, airy office with tall windows that looked to the east and the blue waters of Lake Michigan.

Randolph Littleton did not rise from his desk. He motioned Mary Ellen to a seat and watched her intently as she took out her notebook. "What can I do for you, Miss Selvedge?"

Mary Ellen stared back at him. "I'm here in my capacity as a detective of the Jefferson County Sheriff's Department."

"All right—*Detective* Selvedge. You don't look the part."

"And you don't look like you have ever been down in a coal mine."

Littleton stiffened. "I was never a coal miner. Let's get to the business at hand. Why are you here?"

"We are investigating the possibility that your daughter has simply run off and is now in hiding. I am here to talk to her family and friends to see if they can give us any clues about her state of mind at the time she disappeared."

Littleton jumped to his feet, leaned forward, and put his hands on his desk. "Preposterous! In hiding, you say! Where in God's name did you get that idea?"

"It's one of three possibilities that we have to investigate. At this point, it is looking less likely that she was kidnapped, and there is no evidence of murder."

Littleton sat back in his chair, still angry. "I see. So what do you want to ask me?"

"Was Amanda happily married?"

"How would I know that? She should have been. Newcombe is a promising young man."

"Were you and your daughter close?"

"Not really. I don't see what purpose this line of questions serves. Unless you have some meaningful matters to discuss, I'm afraid . . . "

"Why did you have your company police do surveillance when your daughter was going with Hanley Friedman?"

"I did it with others of her friends. Amanda stands to inherit quite a bit of money some day. I wanted to protect her from fortune hunters."

"Did you force her to marry Newcombe?"

"No, I did not, and I think this interview is about over."

"Do I have your permission to interview your wife and daughter?"

"Yes, for all the good that will do you."

"Mr. Littleton, thank you for your time. I have learned quite a bit."

Littleton buzzed his secretary and said, "Miss Sewell will show you out."

On the cab ride back to her hotel, Mary Ellen was unhappy with her questioning of Littleton. Why had she gone out of her way to make him angry? Was it the remark about not looking like a detective? *For heaven's sake,* she told herself, *don't let your ego get in the way of doing your job. A good detective has to keep everything impersonal.*

She had to admit, however, that she was prepared to dislike Littleton from the beginning. It was his whole attitude toward his daughter. There had been no letters from him in Amanda's desk, and the way Littleton had reacted toward Amanda's romance with Hanley Friedman seemed awfully high handed.   And it was obvious that he had more or less forced Amanda to marry Newcombe. When she had asked if Amanda was happily married, Littleton's answer told a lot. It made it clear he didn't really care whether she was happily married or not—she should have been. Littleton's main concern seemed to be with his personal image. Otherwise, why had he become so upset when she suggested Amanda may be in hiding? *The daughter of a great man like Littleton in hiding rather than kidnapped! That just wouldn't do!*

Somewhere in the process of thinking about Littleton, Mary Ellen reached the conclusion that much of Amanda's rather strange behavior came from the way she had been treated by her father. The bookishness, the withdrawal, the drab clothing—all were indications of a fundamentally unhappy and lonely woman.

Mary Ellen thought about her own father. Art Selvedge was a big-hearted, friendly man. He started working in the mines as a boy and saved enough money to start the City Café by the time he was in his mid thirties. What made the café work was Art's out-going personality—and good food. Mary Ellen was his only child, but he had never spoiled her. He played games with her when she was small, he helped her with her homework in school, and he was proud when she excelled. She had always known that her father loved her. A father like that would never have tried to dictate whom she should marry.

Mary Ellen laughed at herself. *Well, so much for being an impersonal detective. I guess I am going to have to try harder to be objective. But really, being completely impersonal is impossible. In real life, you are what you are, and you can't change that. I'll just have to try to understand who I am and where I'm coming from and what affect that may have on my judgement.*

When Mary Ellen got back to the Bismark Hotel, she made a call to the home of Randolph Littleton and got an appointment to talk with Mrs. Littleton the following morning. That evening, she had dinner in the hotel dining room. No less than three men tried to get acquainted with her, two travelling salesmen and a local politician. She was courteous but not friendly. When the politician introduced himself and asked if he could join her, she answered firmly, "No. I am dining alone."

The Littleton house was on Lake Shore Drive in a stretch of fine homes facing Lake Michigan. The district, according to the cab driver, was known as the Gold Coast. Mary Ellen paid the driver and walked through an iron gate and up stone stairs to the entry of what an architect would have said was an excellent example of a Second Empire chateau, complete with mansard roof and twin columns guarding the entry. A butler answered the door and showed her into the front parlor. Mary Ellen had never seen anything like this except in the movies. Looking at the large oil paintings, French furniture, and marble fireplace, she could imagine Douglas Fairbanks and Norma Shearer in 18th Century costumes playing a romantic scene. She also thought about how this sumptuous dwelling contrasted with the shotgun houses of most coal miners.

After about twenty minutes, a middle-aged woman in a nurses' uniform appeared. "Miss Selvedge, I am Florence Hadley. I take care of Mrs. Littleton. She is ready to see you now."

"Is she ill?"

"No, but she is confined to her rooms most of the time. I've been with the family for years. I take care of all of them." She led Mary Ellen to an upstairs room and announced her to Mrs. Littleton. The room was large and tastefully decorated in soft pastel colors. Mrs. Littleton, in a pale lavender dressing gown, sat on a small French provincial settee with a tiny table in front of her. She had a pale, translucent beauty with an almost sad quality. Through a door opening into the next room, Mary Ellen could see a large bedroom and a canopied bed with lace curtains. There was not a touch of masculinity in the suite of rooms.

Mrs. Littleton reached for the coffee carafe on the small table. "I am Abigail Agnew Littleton, my dear. Would you like coffee?"

Mary Ellen walked to the tiny table accepted a small demitasse of coffee, and took a seat on a padded chair that matched the settee.

"Mrs. Littleton," she began, "I am a detective from Jefferson County working on the case of your missing daughter. I would like to ask you a few questions."

"How on earth can *I* help?"

"We need to know more about your daughter—who her friends were, what her interests were, and particularly if she was happily married."

Mrs. Littleton was so surprised by what Mary Ellen had asked that it was obvious her husband had not briefed her on his interview the day before. She poured herself more coffee before she answered. "I'm afraid I am not a good person to ask those questions. Amanda and I were never close. She was always a bit withdrawn, and then I have been limited in my activities by my health."

She looked perfectly healthy except for an unnatural paleness that was disguised by subtle make-up.

"Well, what kind of girl was she growing up? A tom-boy, studious, adventuresome, shy—any of those?"  In court she would have been accused of leading the witness.

"I suppose two of those—studious and shy."

"Did she have much of a social life?"

"I tried to get her involved. Her sister was a debutante, but Amanda wanted no part of it."

"Do you know why?"

"It's an elaborate process. There are all kinds of preparations that have to be made— photographs, classes in etiquette, dancing, appearance, a complete wardrobe for all occasions, and then there is the coming out party with the proper escort and a suitable gown. Diedra, her sister, did it beautifully. Her picture was on the front page of the *Tribune* society section. But Amanda balked at even beginning the process. She said it was foolishness. I was devastated. She could have done it. She has the possibilities if only she had been willing to develop them."

"Did you approve of her relationship with Hanley Friedman?"

"No."

"What about Richard Newcombe?"

"That's different. She married him."

"Does she love him?"

"Of course."

"Mrs. Littleton, I have to ask this—is it possible that Amanda was unhappy being married to Newcombe and living in a small town in Southern Illinois away from her family and friends?"

"Unhappy? Oh, I suppose most young women go through something like that when they are first married. She never wrote me a single word about being unhappy down there, but then she never wrote me about her personal feelings. That's just the way she always was."

"Well then, I won't take any more of your time. We have not given up hope that your daughter is still alive, and we will keep on working until we find her."

"Thank you, my dear."

Mrs. Littleton rang a small silver bell and Florence Hadley appeared to show her out. When they parted at the front door, Florence put her hand on Mary Ellen's shoulder. "Please find Amanda, Miss Selvedge. She's the best of them."

In the afternoon, Mary Ellen took the elevated train to Wennetka where she had an appointment with Diedra Littleton Northcut, Amanda's older sister. Using a map and directions she got from the friendly hotel clerk, Mary Ellen found the up-scale town house where Diedra lived with her husband, Arthur Northcut, a promising young lawyer. Diedra herself answered the door, explaining that the governess was busy with the two small children. Mary Ellen liked her immediately. She seemed like a more vibrant and engaging version of her mother. She led Mary Ellen to a well-lit and comfortable study, again with a view of the lake. "How can I help?" she asked as they took seats.

As Mary Ellen explained her mission and expressed the idea that Amanda may not have been kidnapped or murdered and that she may have just run away, she watched Diedra closely for her reaction. She seemed to accept the idea that Amanda was still alive as a given, and she was not visibly surprised at the possibility that Amanda had run away.

"So you want to know more about her, is that it?" Diedra said as she poured them both a glass of lemonade.

"That's it, and I have to tell you that there is a lot I have *not* learned from your father and mother."

"That doesn't surprise me. They don't know much about her. She was always a puzzle to them."

"What can you tell me?"

"She never confided in me—not really, but we grew up together. I think I know her pretty well. She is what they call in psychology classes an introvert. She lives in her own world."

"And what's that world like?"

Diedra sipped her lemonade. "It's a world of dreams, of romance and great ideas, and a world that needs to be made better."

"That's why she reads books so much?"

"Right."

"What about making the world better? Is she a New Dealer or a socialist or something like that?

"She's pretty close to being both, but basically she's a liberal. And she doesn't really care about being rich. That's fashionable these days. Have you noticed how many of the villains and bad people in movies are big businessmen? Before the Depression, we admired people like Henry Ford and John D. Rockefeller, but now we blame them for the Depression and we hate them, at least in the movies. And the current writers like Sinclair Lewis and others—they make the rich look foolish and evil. I think Amanda has bought into that kind of thinking."

"Then, what does she think of your father?"

"Oh, she loves him, I suppose—as a father. But she hates the fact that his money comes from exploiting the labor of coal miners who live in near poverty."

"Did she ever actually do anything about her liberal beliefs like join a political party or work for some cause?"

"No. Remember, she's an introvert. She doesn't like getting involved with other people."

Mary Ellen changed the subject. "What about Hanley Friedman? Did she love him?"

"I think she did. He was a lot like her, although he was a little more inclined to get involved in worthy causes."

"Then why did she marry Richard Newcombe?"

"You have to realize the kind of pressures my parents can put. She never wanted to displease them."

"She did exactly that when she refused to be a debutante."

"I suppose I had something to do with that. I went through the whole thing, and while I enjoyed some of it, I knew Amanda would hate it. I told her it was a bunch of silliness. The only purpose was to advertise your wares and catch a rich husband so you could join the high society of Chicago."

Mary Ellen could not resist. "Is that what happened to you?"

"Good Lord, no. Arthur was a struggling law student when we married. His father is a railroad conductor. Believe me—my parents were not happy when I married him.

"He seems to be doing well now."

"He's a very good lawyer."

"And Richard Newcombe—what do you think of him?"

"I don't know much about him. Amanda never talked about him, and I have really been around him very little. He likes to flirt—that's about my only impression."

"One more question. Do you know anything about the code that Amanda used in writing letters to Hanley Friedman?"

"Code? No, I don't know anything about that. I was married and gone from the house when that affair was going on. But you might check the writing desk in her room. Mrs. Hadley keeps her room exactly the way it was when she lived there. It's like a museum."

"Well, that's about all the questions I have. I want to thank you for your frank answers. You have made my job much easier."

Mary Ellen started to rise, but Diedra lifted her hand. "So since we have had this nice girl-to-girl talk, I would like to ask you a question—a personal one."

Mary Ellen was surprised but curious. "OK, what is it?"

"I noticed you are not wearing a ring. How did a lovely thing like you avoid getting married up 'til now? What's wrong with the men down in Southern Illinois?"

"Oh, they're quite normal, I guess. I just haven't found the right one."

"And how did you become a sheriff's detective?"

"Actually, I run a café. I talked the sheriff into letting me be a part-time detective because that's what I really want to do in life."

"This sheriff—is he young? And is he married?"

"Yes and no."

"I think I have the picture now."

As she showed Mary Ellen to the door, Diedra put an arm around her shoulders and said, "The next time you are in Chicago, I want you to call me. We'll get together and have lunch, maybe a cocktail."

Mary Ellen smiled. "I'd like that."

"Good, I want to know how it comes out with you and your sheriff."

What she had learned from Diedra convinced Mary Ellen she had to know more about Hanley Friedman. A call to Chief Kelly yielded the names and address of Hanley's parents, Simon and Madelyn, who lived on the Near North Side. Thinking that an unannounced visit for an interview might get a better response, Mary Ellen boarded the El and, with the help of her map, found her way to the address. The Friedmans lived in a two-story brownstone with a tree lined brick sidewalk out front. A wrought iron fence and gate guarded their front yard, which was about the size of a billiard table. Mary Ellen rang the doorbell and almost immediately the door swung open to reveal a small, trim woman with black hair and large brown eyes.

"Mrs. Friedman?" Mary Ellen asked.

"Yes."

"I am Detective Mary Ellen Selvedge." She showed her badge. "I am in Chicago investigating the disappearance of Amanda Newcombe. You may have read about it."

"Amanda? Yes . . . of course I have read about it. It's awful. Such a nice, refined young woman."

"Then you have met her?"

"Certainly. My son, Hanley, brought her here several times. Please come in, Detective. I'll help if I can."

She opened the door wide to let Mary Ellen enter. Then she pointed the way to a sitting room with a bay window that looked out over the tiny front yard and the street outside. Mary Ellen was struck instantly by the comfort and good taste of the room. It was anything but sterile, but finding a speck of dirt would have required a magnifying glass.

As Mary Ellen sat down on the Davenport, Mrs. Friedman said, "I was just having a cup of tea. Would you like one?"

Mary Ellen nodded and Mrs. Friedman disappeared, only to return quickly with a tea service and some cookies. As she poured she asked, "How can I help?"

"You say your son brought Amanda here several times. Was that for dinner?"

"Yes. Once. The other times she just came to visit."

"And was it more or less like a son bringing his sweetheart home to meet his family?"

"Yes. I suppose it was."

"Then, did you have the impression that your son and Amanda were thinking about getting married."

"Well, they never said that in so many words, but that was the impression we had."

"What was your reaction to that?"

"Amanda is a lovely young woman—well educated, cultured. We—my husband and I—were delighted."

"Do you have any other children?"

"No. Just Hanley."

"Do you hear from him often?"

"Oh yes. He writes every week. He's teaching in a CCC Camp down south."

"Yes. I know. I met him a few days ago."

"Was he all right? Did he look thin? He never eats the way he should. I worry about him."

"He looked fine. I don't remember him looking thin. Has he been back to visit you since he started his job with the CCC?"

"Only once."

"Mrs. Friedman, we learned that Hanley often leaves the camp on weekends. Do you know where he goes?"

"No. Probably to someplace where they have a good library. He loves to read."

"One more question. When Hanley and Amanda broke up—you know, decided not to get married—whose idea was it?"

"We never knew. He just came home one day and said it was all over."

"How did it affect him?"

"I think he was devastated. He loved her."

"And you and your husband? What was your reaction?"

"We were beginning to love her too. We wanted what was best for both of them, and frankly we never knew why they broke up. It was very sad."

Mary Ellen finished her tea and closed her notebook.

"Have I helped, Miss Selvedge? Anything I can do to help find Amanda alive and safe . . ."

"Mrs. Friedman, you have been very helpful. I want to thank you."

As she walked past the tiny yard and through the gate, Mary Ellen thought that if Madelyn Friedman was a true example, all of the jokes about Jewish mothers were pretty misguided. Anyone would be lucky to have a mother like Madelyn.

Mary Ellen decided to spend one more day in Chicago and go back to the Littleton's Gold Coast home to see what she could find in Amanda's bedroom. Mrs. Hadley met her at the door and showed her to the room. It was not very different from Amanda's room in the house in Zeigler—rather plain with lots of books and not much that revealed personality. Mary Ellen checked the closet and found little there. Her interest went immediately to the writing desk. She found only ordinary papers, but there was a small middle drawer that was locked.

"Do you know where the key is?" she asked Mrs. Hadley.

When the answer was no, Mary Ellen fashioned a pick with a paper clip and picked the tiny lock. "Good heavens!" Mrs. Hadley gasped. "You shouldn't do that! You're invading her privacy."

"It may help us find her," replied Mary Ellen.

When she opened the drawer, it was empty, but as she pulled it out further it came completely out of its slot. *Why lock an empty drawer?* She asked herself. She turned the drawer over and saw a card taped to the bottom. On it were two columns, one with the alphabet and the other with corresponding letters scrambled. It had to be Amanda's secret code. With Mrs. Hadley's permission, she carefully tore the card off of the drawer and put it in her purse.

Satisfied that she had made a valuable discovery, Mary Ellen thanked Mrs. Hadley for her help and went back to her hotel. She was disappointed that there had been no letters in the writing desk to decode, but Marcus had taken dozens of them as evidence in the investigation. When she got back to Franklin, she would begin decoding them.

Mary Elllen checked out of the hotel, and, after sending a telegram telling Marcus when she would arrive at DuQuoin, she caught the afternoon train to Southern Illinois. On the train, she went over what she had learned in Chicago. Neither of Amanda's parents knew much about her—certainly not on any deeply personal level. It was likely that she still loved Hanley Friedman, and it was obvious that she and Richard Newcombe were poorly matched. He was an ambitious climber who probably thought it had been necessary to marry Amanda to advance his career. She was a misfit in the family of a wealthy industrialist and had likely been miserable married to Newcombe, who she may have considered her intellectual inferior. Madelyn Friedman had seemed more motherly toward Amanda than her own mother, and her sister, Diedra, was the only person with any idea of what Amanda was really like. Curiously, Diedra was not noticeably worried about Amanda's welfare. Maybe she knew something she was not revealing, or maybe she simply suspected a circumstance that, if true, would mean that Amanda was still alive. The letters—Amanda's letters from Hanley Friedman—would surely be very revealing when they were decoded. That was the first thing Mary Ellen would work on when she got home.

# CHAPTER 14

The director of the Illinois Office of Mine Safety denied Richard Newcombe's request for a mine rescue team to enter the sealed section of Consolidated Coal's No. 3 Mine at Zeigler. He turned it down flatly, telling Newcombe on the long distance phone that since there were no miners in need of rescue, he could not authorize the use of a rescue team. Newcombe promptly reported the refusal to Marcus, saying it was about what he had expected. It was also what Marcus had expected from Newcombe, since he obviously had no desire to close down the mine and send a team into the abandoned area. Marcus was not sure exactly why Newcombe felt that way, but it was suspicious.

Marcus got the director's name and number from Newcombe and set Sgt. Bailey to work placing a call to the Office of Mine Safety in Springfield. The call had to go through several operators and a switchboard, but finally Bailey had the director on the line. His name was Lester Monroe.

"Mr. Monroe, this is Sheriff Marcus Dixon down in Jefferson County. I want to ask you to reconsider your decision to deny the use of a mine rescue team in a Consolidated Coal mine at Zeigler."

"Yes, I remember the request. You have to understand, Sheriff, those teams are for rescue work only. They are well trained, but it is a highly dangerous thing to go into a closed section of a mine, and I cannot authorize it unless lives are actually at stake."

"A life may be at stake, Mr. Monroe. We are involved down here in a possible kidnapping or murder investigation. You may have read about it."

"Is that the case of the missing coal heiress? I read that the FBI had entered the case."

"That's it. We have no solid evidence to indicate what has happened to her, but we have a report that a body may have been thrown down the air shaft of the mine we want to enter. It would help our investigation a great deal if we could determine for sure whether there's a body down there and who it is. If it's Mrs. Newcombe, we can concentrate on the murder investigation, but if it's not her it would mean she could still be alive and we would have to pursue other avenues."

"Did you say her name was Newcombe? That was the name of the mine manager that called me."

"The missing woman is his wife."

"Well, he didn't tell me that. In fact, he didn't tell me most of what you just have. He really didn't make a very strong case."

Marcus thought for a moment: should he reveal that Newcombe was a suspect? He had not given that information to the press, but revealing it might persuade Monroe.

"Newcombe is a suspect, Mr. Monroe. We think he may be involved in his wife's disappearance."

"Hmm. I suppose if that's the way it is, I could reconsider. I'll tell you what Sheriff—I'll authorize the use of one of our teams as long as the members volunteer for the search. I'll let you know sometime tomorrow if one of the teams is willing to do it."

"Thank you, sir. I was hoping that once you learned the full facts, you might change your mind."

Late the next afternoon, Marcus got a call from the leader of the mine rescue team stationed in Herrin. His name was Bill Welker, but he said everyone called him "Pistol." He and his team were willing to do the search. Marcus called Newcombe and persuaded him to close the mine on the coming Sunday so the search could be done. He then called Pistol Welker and told him to have his team at No. 3 Mine by 9 o'clock Sunday morning.

Welker came to Zeigler on Saturday and spent the day working with Newcombe, the mine supervisor, the mine engineer, and others, making sure all the necessary preparations were in place. No one was to be in any part of the mine on Sunday except for the rescue team and those working with them. The ventilation system was to be operating fully, the mine lights were to be on, but there was to be no open flame and no equipment operating that might produce an electric spark. Welker himself went into the mine to check for methane gas at the stopping, the concrete block wall that sealed the opening to the closed section.

From Maureen Zalesky in the company office, Welker obtained a map of the closed section. It showed that the air shaft was at the far end of the section, a distance of several hundred yards through passages cut in the coal seam. In this part of the mine, the seam of coal, Illinois Number 4, was about eight feet thick and had been mined out in a grid of corridors leaving perhaps a third of the coal still in place to hold up the roof. The problem for the team would be finding their way through the maze of corridors and squares in the complete dark. The corridors were numbered on the map, and Welker was confident they would be marked, but the markings would be very difficult to find in the dark. Also, it would be too risky to turn on the old lighting system in the closed section. Any kind of electrical short or exploding light bulb would almost certainly cause an explosion.

The threat was methane gas. Colorless, odorless, and highly flammable, methane exists naturally in many rock formations. Any disturbance of the formations causes the gas to seep out, making it one of the worst hazards of underground mining. Breathing methane is not toxic, although strong concentrations can cause asphyxiation. The gas is lighter than air and accumulates near the ceiling of the mine. It could be detected by hand-held sensors used by mine inspectors.

Methane provides the fuel for the worst of all mine disasters—fire or explosion. When that happens, the immediate hazard is carbon monoxide, a toxic gas produced by the incomplete combustion of methane or coal dust, the other possible fuel always present in a mine. The great amounts of CO gas produced in a mine fire or explosion are enough to be fatal to those who breathe it.

Welker anticipated that in addition to difficulties the team would have finding their way in the complete darkness, moving down the corridors was not going to be a walk in the park. There had probably been roof falls, which would fill passages with debris, perhaps even close them. There would also be water in low places. There was a real risk of the team getting separated or members getting lost. Communication was always a problem. Welker planned to use a life line that ran from him as the leader to the last man, but experience had taught him to make sure that the members of the team along the line were not tied securely to it. If they were, one member falling might pull all of the others down. The life line needed to pass through a ring on each member's belt so he could move freely. Also, there needed to be a light strip or reflector on the back of each member's helmet so the man behind him could see him.

Marcus and Mary Ellen were waiting at the entry to Mine No.3 when the rescue team arrived in a truck. Richard Newcombe was also there, obviously not prepared to go anywhere near the mine since he was dressed in a sport coat, white shirt, and knit tie. Also there were Mike Hardesty, the mine supervisor, and Otis Hatcher, the mine engineer, both dressed to go down into the mine. They had recruited three coal miners who would use pneumatic drills and sledge hammers to break through the stopping.

The five-man rescue team dismounted from the truck and lined up in a military rank. They wore yellow coats, white protective helmets, and all had belt packs which contained first aid kits, lights, knives, and hand picks. On their backs were pressure tanks containing compressed air. The tanks had regulator valves which allowed air to flow through a flexible hose to their face masks.

After introductions all around, Marcus explained the mission to the team. As he spoke his eyes went from one team member to the other. He found himself thinking what a fine looking group they were—clear-eyed, no sign of fear, all in their thirties or early forties, and obviously in good physical condition.

Pistol Welker stepped forward and asked who else was going into the mine. Newcombe pointed to Hardesty and Hatcher and the three miners. "Good, we'll need you two to guide us to the stopping and help open it."

"I'm going also," said Marcus.

"And me," added Mary Ellen.

Everyone looked shocked. Welker glanced at Mary Ellen and shook his head.

"Detective Selvedge, as much as we would like to have your company, it just won't do for you to go. A woman in a coal mine—that's very bad luck. And we're going to need all the good luck we can get on this one."

Mary Ellen looked disappointed but said nothing.

"I'd like to go into the closed area with you," Marcus said. "Do you have an extra outfit for me? If there is a body in there, I will need to get a look at it, and take some pictures."

"I appreciate that, Sheriff, but this job takes a lot of training, and you might become a hindrance for us. And taking pictures—well we sure as hell can't have any flash bulbs going off in there. You can't understand how damned dark it is until you have experienced it. There just wouldn't be enough light to take any pictures. Now, if we find a body, we plan to bring it out on a stretcher. We're trained to do that."

Marcus nodded, and Welker continued. "Now, here's the plan: when we break through the stopping, we're probably going to release some methane into the mine. We'll make the hole small and down low so as to keep the flow to a minimum. When we break through, all of you except the team should withdraw forty or fifty feet up the corridor that the air is coming from. The ventilation system will start drafting some of the gas and air out of the closed area, but if you're up the corridor it will carry it away from you. When we come out, we will close the hole, and the fans will clear the methane out of the mine if they are run continuously for about twelve hours. That way, the mine can go back to work on Monday. The state inspectors will have to clear it, but you fellows know how that works."

With that, the team, Marcus, Hardesty, Hatcher, and the three miners loaded their equipment into the rail car that would carry them down into the mine. After they left, there was an awkward moment when Mary Ellen and Richard Newcombe looked at each other. Then, Newcombe said, "This will take hours. Let's go over to the supervisor's office and wait there."

The supervisor's office was a stark contrast to the company offices Mary Ellen had seen in Chicago. The walls were bare wood, decorated only by several tattered safety posters and a calendar provided by a local mechanic's shop and featuring a picture of a buxom girl in a bathing suit. A coal-burning iron stove stood next to one wall, unused in the summer weather. The only other amenities were an electric hot plate and a chipped blue enamel coffee pot. Mary Ellen found a tin of coffee, drew water at the faucet in the blackened wash basin, and made coffee. When it was done, she poured the brew into two tin cups she had washed in the basin.

Newcombe accepted the coffee, leaned back in one of the two wooden chairs, and tried to start a conversation. "So, I understand you visited Chicago, and you talked with several of my in-laws."

Mary Ellen was not interested in getting cozy with Newcombe, but she wanted very much to get a better reading on what he was thinking at that moment. He seemed way too relaxed for a man who had thrown his wife down an air shaft and knew she was about to be found. In fact, he did not seem nervous at all.

"That's right. I talked with your father-in-law and mother-in-law and with your sister-in-law."

"Quite an interesting family, aren't they? Everyone's very different." Mary Ellen agreed.

"Did you learn anything from them that will help find Amanda?"

"I may have. She is certainly a different person from the other members of the family."

"Yes, it's hard to believe that they *are* her family."

Mary Ellen looked at him closely. She had not expected such frankness.

"Do you think she was happy?"

"Happy? Well, I suppose so. She had a nice life here. I know it's not the Gold Coast, but she had a fine house, a housekeeper, an expensive car—everything she needed."

"She didn't seem to have any friends."

"No, I don't either. These are just not our kind of people down here in Southern Illinois."

"Why do you say that?"

Realizing he had sounded snobbish, Newcombe tried to retreat into generalities. "Oh, it's more than just the big city-small town sort of thing. The people down here really seem to resent anyone from Chicago. They live their small town lives, raise their families, gossip about their neighbors, and basically just try to get by. A big cultural event is going to a movie or something called a bully fight. If it's the Italians it's some kind of festival. The Bohunks have a wurstfest. They have no idea of what goes on in the outside world. They don't even have a public library in any of these coal towns. Nobody is trying to get ahead. Very few of them ever go to college or even think about getting away from here to find a better life. As long as the men can go fishing and hunting and earn enough to provide for their families, they are happy. No ambition! And the way they dress—most of them don't even own a suit of clothes. Worst of all is the Southern Illinois accent—it's straight out of the Kentucky hills. They sound like hillbillies."

By the time he ended his tirade, Mary Ellen was getting faintly amused—and offended. "Well, you certainly don't think much of us," she said in mock dismay.

"Good God. I'm not talking about you! None of that applies to you. You are one of the most attractive . . . ."

She did not let him finish. "You were speaking generally, I suppose."

"Yeah. Generally. Didn't you see the difference when you went to Chicago?"

"Yes, there is certainly a big difference. But you don't seem to realize that people can have all kinds of ambition, but if there are no opportunities for them to get ahead, they just can't do it. If your coal company paid the miners better, they could afford to have a library in their town, and they could send their children to college."

"I'm not sure that's true. Most of them would just spend their money on beer and hunting rifles—and cars. They all want cars."

Mary Ellen could tell that Newcombe's shell of conservatism was hard. It was a sharp contrast to his wife's way of thinking, so she decided to explore that. She remarked, "Amanda's sister seems to believe that Amanda is a liberal—someone who would want to do more to help coal miners improve themselves and the lives of their families."

"You're telling me! She was on me all the time about that sort of thing. It was about the only thing she was willing to talk about. But that was as far as it went. When I told her she could go get into some kind of do-gooder work, you know, like volunteering at a hospital or maybe church work, she would just retreat to her room and write letters or read books. Some liberal! Like most of them, she was all talk."

"You keep using the past tense. Do you believe she is dead?"

"Lord, I don't know.  I hope to God she isn't. It's almost like the best thing we can hope for is that she has been kidnapped and is still alive."

"Have you ever thought that she might just have run off?"

"Run off? Where to? Who with?"

"With another man."

Newcombe laughed. "You know, I don't think she has the nerve for that."

The search party reached the stopping in about twenty minutes. True to Pistol Welker's instructions, the electric lights in the mine were on, the ventilation system was operating, and there was no one in the mine but them. Welker surveyed the situation, tested the direction the air was moving, and chose the place in the concrete block wall where the hole was to be made. The three miners set to work with their drill and sledge hammers breaking through the wall while the rescue team put on their gear and attached their life line. The experienced miners made quick work of knocking a hole in the stopping. It was only about five feet high and three feet wide, but that was the plan.

Pistol motioned for Marcus and the two others to move up the corridor from which the air was coming, and after his team checked their equipment, turned on their lights, opened their air regulators, and put on their masks he led them through the hole and into the abandoned area.

Marcus, Supervisor Hardesty, and Engineer Hatcher found places to sit on wooden benches in a break area and began their wait. Hatcher produced a large thermos of coffee and shared it with the others.

"Have either of you ever worked in that area?" Marcus asked.

"Yeah, years ago," Hardesty answered.

"What's it like in there?"

"Oh, about like any other. You've got a pretty decent overhead—seven or eight feet, and the coal in that area was pretty good, not a lot of rock. The overhead is held up with roof bolts and steel plates, but I expect there have been quite a few roof falls."

Hatcher added, "Always was a lot of water in that part of the mine.

We had to pump it out fairly often. But nothing came out when they opened the hole, so that's a good sign."

Marcus commented, "You know, you have to admire those rescue guys. It must take good training and a whole lot of guts to do what they do."

Both men nodded. "You can say that again," Hardesty commented. "There's nobody we admire more than those guys. Today is a picnic compared to what they face when they go into a mine where there has been a major collapse or an explosion. When anything like that happens, they go in—and sometimes they don't come out. Well, I'll take that back. We never leave anyone in a mine. We always get them out eventually, but I meant sometimes they don't come out alive."

"Yeah, it takes a special kind of man to be on one of those rescue teams," Hatcher added. "I've known several guys who decided they wanted to try it. The job sounds good at first. They thought they wouldn't have to go down in the mines every day—they would just sit around and wait to be called. But that's not the way it is. They train a lot, and the training is realistic. Some of the guys had to give it up when they panicked on an exercise or got lost and had to be rescued themselves."

"You think it will be difficult for them today?"

"Well, it won't be easy. The darkness, the debris, the water, and the gas—they have to deal with all of that, plus they only have so much air. They may try to operate without the masks if it takes too long to get to the air shaft. The closer they get to the shaft, the better their air supply will be with the ventilation system sucking air through the shaft."

The conversation went on for almost three hours. Both Hardesty and Hatcher proved to be good story tellers, and Marcus held his own. Marcus learned more than he had ever wanted to know about coal mining, but the talk helped pass the time. Finally, around one o'clock, they could hear sounds coming from the hole in the stopping. They moved up to the hole and helped the weary rescue team climb through the hole with their equipment.

Pistol Welker took off his helmet and mask and looked strangely at Marcus. "You ain't going to believe this, Sheriff, but there's four dead bodies at the bottom of that air shaft."

"Four!"

"Yeah, that's right. And none of 'em are women."

"You sure?"

"Well, two of them had been down there for a long time—pretty decomposed, but all four were wearing men's clothing. We didn't bother to check any further than that. All four have been shot. There were bullet holes in their clothes, and one had one in his head. Two of them had their hands and feet tied. "

"And you didn't bring any of them out?"

"We couldn't see the point. We went in there to see if there was a woman's body, and there wasn't one."

Marcus thought for a moment. "Right. . . . No way to bring out four bodies. Well, I want to thank you fellows. You did a great job."

When Marcus told Newcombe and Mary Ellen what the team had found, Newcombe took it in stride. He seemed relieved that his wife had not been found—at least not found dead at the bottom of an air shaft in a coal mine.

On the way back to Franklin, Mary Ellen asked Marcus what he was going to do about the four dead bodies.

He answered, "That old air shaft has become a dump for murder victims. This is probably gang stuff. It may be where some of the Shelton's enemies have ended up, or they may be members of the Shelton gang. Either way, it's murder, and we are going to have to look into it."

"That would mean getting those bodies out of there, but how can we do that?"

"I'll get in touch with the state police and the state crime lab and probably the FBI. Maybe they will have some way to help. It may take a court order to get anything done."

Mary Ellen folded her hands in her lap. "I'm glad Amanda wasn't down there. I was afraid she might be. But now—well, maybe she is still alive."

# CHAPTER 15

Decoding the forty-three letters Marcus had collected from Amanda Newcombe's bedroom desk was laborious. Mary Ellen had to transpose each letter, using the code she had found on the bottom of the small drawer in Amanda's desk at the Littleton home in Chicago. She worked on the task for two days. Finally, when she had finished, it was past nine o'clock at night, but she had to tell Marcus what she had learned. She walked the few blocks from her house to the Court House. Wilford Simpson, sitting at the sergeant's desk in the Sheriff's Office, was surprised to see her. When she asked for Marcus, Simpson said he was upstairs in his apartment, "probably listening to the Cardinal game."

"Do you want me to call him down here?" Simpson asked.

"No, just tell me how to get up there. I've got some interesting letters to show him."

"OK, but I'd better warn him you are coming." Simpson flipped the switch on the intercom and spoke into it: "Mary Ellen is coming up to see you, Sheriff. She has some letters to show you."

"Tell her to wait a few minutes. I've got to get some clothes on."

"I wonder what he's wearing now," Mary Ellen laughed.

"Oh, he lounges around in his shorts up there—doesn't have many callers. You sure you want to go up there? He could come down here."

"I've always wanted to see where he lives. Is it a nice apartment?"

"Nah. There's nothing in this whole court house you could call nice. It's decent, but I wouldn't want to live there very long. Come with me and I'll put you on the elevator to go up.  He should be ready by now. ”

When the elevator door opened, Mary Ellen walked into the jail area and, following Simpson's instructions, asked the desk officer how to get to the sheriff's apartment. The startled officer could hardly speak. Catcalls and whistles came from the cell area.

"Whooee!" one of the prisoners yelled. "Looks like the sheriff is going to get some tonight!"

"Pipe down in there," the jailer warned. "She's a detective. She might arrest you."

"We're already arrested, butt hole,"

"Sorry, Miss," the jailer grinned. "We don't get many visitors like you up here."

"It's OK. Now, which way is the sheriff's apartment?"

Marcus opened the door for Mary Ellen when she knocked. It did not take her long to confirm Deputy Simpson's assessment of the sheriff's quarters. To say they were Spartan would have been generous.

Marcus watched Mary Ellen survey the place. "Like it?" he asked.

"Well, it certainly is . . . uh, plain."

"It's also free, so I don't complain. Come into the kitchen. We can sit at the table. Want some coffee? I've got a pot here I could heat up."

Mary Ellen looked at the battered aluminum coffee pot and shook her head. "I brought some of Hanley Friedman's letters that I have decoded. I'm not sure what to make of them."

She laid about a dozen letters on the table and Marcus picked up one. He read it carefully and then peered over it at Mary Ellen. "He's sure as hell in love with her, isn't he?"

"No doubt about that. It's in all of his letters."

"So what is it you want to show me?"

"In several letters, he talks about the last time they met. There's no way to know when or where that was, but he says in one letter something about executing 'our plan.'  What do you suppose that means?"

"Does he mention their plan anywhere else?"

"No."

"Then we don't have much to go on, do we?"

"Do you think their plan could have anything to do with her disappearance?"

"I think it's a pretty good bet."

"So what do you want to do?"

"First thing is to tell the FBI about these letters. They may have some ideas."

Mary Ellen stood and walked over to the stove and felt the coffee pot. She decided it was warm enough to drink. She sensed that Marcus was staring at her as she poured two cups of coffee. She had worn a gauzy summer dress that fitted perfectly. Her hair, so often worn up, now flowed down to her shoulders. She moved easily, almost languidly. With a cup of coffee in each hand, she turned slowly to see that Marcus was watching intently.

She handed Marcus the coffee and took her seat again. "Marcus," she said softly. "I think we need to look some more at Hanley Friedman."

Marcus stirred in his seat. "Huh . . . oh yeah. Right. We need to look some more at Hanley—but look at what specifically?"

"Remember, the camp commander at the CCC camp told us that he goes into town on weekends. I'd like to know exactly where he goes."

Marcus nodded. "The commander said they send a truck into Carbondale for the corpsmen, and didn't he tell us that Friedman usually rides with them?"

"Yes. So we need to know where and when that truck lets people off in Carbondale."

"So we can follow Friedman and see where he goes?"

"Exactly," Mary Ellen smiled. "That shouldn't be too hard to do."

"OK. I'll call the CCC camp in the morning and find out about the truck."

Marcus started to rise, saying, "Anything else?"

"Marcus, I want to talk about something."

He sank back in his chair, looking a bit uncomfortable. "OK, what is it?"

"I'm getting discouraged about this case. We don't seem to be getting anywhere. It has been three weeks since Amanda disappeared, and we still don't have a clear picture of what happened to her."

Marcus nodded. "I've been a bit discouraged too. But we have to realize that we're not a big police force. It's not like in the movies where they solve the crime by the end of the show.  Altogether, here in Jefferson County we have . . . let's see, about twenty-five or thirty town policemen in the four communities that are large enough to have a police department. Then there are four small town marshals. My department has five deputies, one sergeant, five jailors, and one detective—you. We are all there is to enforce the law in this county, and we have to do it around the clock, twenty-four hours a day, seven days a week. We can call in the state police for help on big cases that overlap other counties, but the basic responsibility for handling cases like murder and kidnapping falls on the local police, and in this county it is mostly on me. You are the only detective in the county. We have no crime lab, no county-wide communication system, and, in fact, the old 19th Century laws and antiquated court system are pretty damned hard to deal with in the first place."

He took a drink of coffee and looked at Mary Ellen. She sat with her hands folded, listening closely. Her eyes glistened.

"The truth is," Marcus continued, "that a rural county like this is a good place to commit a murder or kidnapping. There's a better chance of getting away with it. If it's a kidnapping, we can call in the FBI, but I have to say they don't seem very effective. They get a lot of publicity for gang busting and that sort of thing, but I haven't been impressed with what they have done in our case. I got a report yesterday from Sheriff Braxton down in Williamson County. He says the FBI is making very little progress in tracking down the other people who were involved in the attempted extortion and they can't get Henry Pfister to talk—he was the guy who kidnapped you. They are going to prosecute Pfister in Williamson County, but I don't look for much more to be done down there, either by the FBI or the sheriff. So here we are, trying to solve a big murder or kidnapping case, with the newspapers and wire services breathing down our necks every day, and we haven't got a whole lot of tools to work with."

Mary Ellen said, "Marcus, I am afraid I am one of the tools that hasn't been working very well. Do you regret making me a detective?"

"Why are you asking?"

"Well, I'm trying real hard to do well at this, and I guess I just need a little encouragement."

"Haven't I been encouraging enough?"

Tears now showed in Mary Ellen's eyes. "No. Not really."

"Aw hell, I'm sorry. Of course I don't regret making you a detective. You have been a great help. You have good ideas, you work well with people, and you have courage. I worried a lot about you—you know—your safety when you went to Chicago, but you did a good job up there. In fact, you may have turned up something that could break this case. So don't feel bad."

He handed her his handkerchief.

"Besides, I like having you around. I like that a lot. In fact, it's becoming a problem for me. I'm afraid my feelings for you are getting to be a lot more than official."

Mary Ellen looked up, her face radiant.

"Oh Marcus, when you kissed me that time, I . . . ."

Marcus came around the table and took her in his arms. She raised her face and closed her eyes. When Marcus kissed her, he could feel her heart pounding against his chest. The taste of her lips made his breath come fast. They held each other sensing the moment—the scent of her hair, the strength of his arms, the swell of her breasts, the hardness of his body.

Finally, Marcus gently pushed her away. "You had better go now," he said, his voice breaking.

"Wha . . . What's wrong?"

"Mary Ellen, if you stay now, you know what will happen."

"Is that so bad?"

" No. It would be what I want, but this is a small town. If you stay here tonight, it will be all over town tomorrow."

She knew he was right, but she didn't care. "I want to stay. I love you. There, I've said it."

Marcus put his arms around her. "Mary Ellen, I think I have loved you ever since we said goodbye at the train, but I just didn't know if you . . . well, anyhow, let's play this by the book. We'll get engaged, and we'll do all that other stuff, you know, send out announcements and get married and all that."

"That's not much of a proposal, Marcus, but I accept."

She took his hand and started toward the bedroom. "Now that we're engaged . . ."

They moved a few steps but then Marcus stopped. He took her by the shoulders, kissed her softly, and turned her toward the front door. "Mary Ellen," he said, "we're going to have a great marriage. Let's do this whole thing right." He picked up his hat and gun belt and led her through the jail section, past the hoots and catcalls of the prisoners, and into the elevator.

"It's almost midnight. I'm going to walk you home."

Mary Ellen's head was spinning as they rode in the elevator. There was no doubt about it—Marcus really loved her. She understood why he was determined to "do this whole thing right." He did not want to treat her like another one night stand. He had respect for her. He wanted their marriage to be perfect.

Early Saturday morning, Marcus picked up Mary Ellen at her home and they drove to Carbondale. From his inquiries at the CCC camp, Marcus had learned that the weekend pass truck arrived in Carbondale about 8:30 in the morning, and that all passengers got off at the Illinois Central Railroad Station on South Illinois Street. Across Illinois Street from the train station was a popular eating place named the Corner Café. The café had two large windows that faced the station. By 8:00 a.m., Marcus and Mary Ellen were having breakfast at a table where they had a view of the small parking lot of the train station. They had just finished eating when the CCC truck arrived. About twenty uniformed corpsmen jumped off the truck and went their separate ways. More than half of them went into the train station to wait for a north-bound train. Two passengers on the truck rode in the cab with the driver. One of them was Hanley Friedman. Dressed in a brown suit and carrying a small canvas bag, he got out of the cab, said something to the driver, and began walking south on Illinois Avenue.

Marcus had already paid the bill for breakfast. He and Mary Ellen quickly left the café and started walking south on the opposite side of the street. They could see Hanley about a block ahead. He went one more block and then crossed the street in front of them and headed west on Poplar Street. Marcus and Mary Ellen had not expected the turn, and when Hanley passed in front of them less than a block away they ducked into the storefront of a shoe store to avoid being seen. Hanley continued down Poplar Street for a block and a half. Rather than follow him, Marcus stood on the corner of Illinois Street and pretended to be talking with Mary Ellen. From his position, he could see when Hanley entered a large two-story apartment house. Once he was inside, Marcus and Mary Ellen walked to the building and went up the same steps Hanley had used. They found themselves in a long central hall that ran the length of the building. On the left was a stairway and on the right a row of eight mailboxes inset in the wall-papered wall.

Mary Ellen checked the names on the mailboxes—no Friedman, no Newcombe, no Littleton. Indeed, there seemed to be nothing but married couples, except for one single person, a M.A. Hawthorne. She pointed at it and said, "Marcus, let's check out Apartment No.7."

They knocked on the door of No.7 several times, but no one answered. They could hear someone moving around inside, so they waited and knocked again. Finally, the door opened a few inches and the face of Hanley Friedman peered out at them.

"It's me, Friedman, Sheriff Dixon. Detective Selvedge and I want to talk with you."

"It's not a good time. Come back later."

"No. Now."

"All right, I'll come out."

He opened the door enough to slide out, but Marcus put his hands on his shoulders and pushed him back into the apartment. Mary Ellen followed.

"What the hell!" Hanley exclaimed. "You can't just shove a man around like that. And you're entering my apartment without my permission."

"The mailbox downstairs says this is the apartment of M.A. Hawthorne," said Mary Ellen.

"Yeah, that's right. He's my roommate. The place is in his name."

"Where is Mr. Hawthorne?" Marcus inquired evenly.

"He's not here. He's a student at the university. He's in class."

"Class on a Saturday morning? He must have a strange schedule." Marcus observed.

Mary Ellen surveyed the apartment. It was neat and well kept, not the look of bachelor quarters. There was a well-arranged kitchen on the right and a room to the left with a closed door, obviously the bedroom. She walked toward the door and reached for the door knob.

"You can't go in there," Hanley's voice became shrill.

"Go ahead, Detective," Marcus said.

Hanley lunged toward Mary Ellen, but Marcus was ready. He stepped in the way and pushed him back.

The door to the bedroom was locked from the inside. Marcus held Hanley by the upper arms and looked him in the eyes. Almost gently, he said, "Tell whoever is in there that he—or she—has to open the door."

"No, you can't do this. We have a right to privacy. You don't have a search warrant. This is all illegal, and I am going to sue you."

Marcus' hands tightened. "Look Hanley, this is either a murder or a kidnapping investigation. You will do yourself a favor if you cooperate. I think I know who is behind that door, and if you try to stop me from finding out, I am going to charge you with obstruction of justice, impeding a police investigation and maybe some other stuff. You will be spending the next several months in the Jefferson County jail."

"All right. All right. But there's been no murder and no kidnapping."

Hanley walked to the door and put his head against it. "Unlock the door, Amanda. We knew this would happen eventually."

There was a sound of the night lock turning, and the door opened. Amanda Newcombe stood with a bewildered look, her hands clutched together.

Mary Ellen moved to her side and put an arm around her. "Are you all right?" she asked, thinking that she looked scared but unharmed.

"I'm all right. Who are you?"

"I'm Mary Ellen. I've been working with the sheriff to try to find you."

"You know who I am?"

"You are Amanda Newcombe, aren't you?"

Amanda ducked her head and nodded.

"All right," Marcus ordered, "everybody sit down in here and let's get to the bottom of this."

Amanda and Hanley sat on a couch. Marcus and Mary Ellen pulled up kitchen chairs and faced them.

"You two have a whole lot of explaining to do," Marcus began. He looked at Amanda, "Why have you been hiding out here when you had to know that the police and FBI are looking for you? The newspapers have been full of how you may have been kidnapped or murdered, and it's been on the radio."

"We just wanted to be together," Hanley explained plaintively.

"Together! Hell man, you ran off with another man's wife!"

"She wants to get a divorce."

Mary Ellen said, "Then she should have done that first. Do you realize how much trouble you have caused?"

"I don't think we have broken any laws," Hanley argued.

"I'll be the judge of that," Marcus said. "I want you to start at the beginning and tell us exactly what you have done, beginning with you" (pointing to Amanda).

Amanda looked at Hanley. He took her hand and held it.

"I never wanted to marry Richard. My parents wanted me to do it so he would make me an acceptable husband and live in Chicago someday and be a part of the rich society there, but I didn't want that. I always loved Hanley, but they didn't think he was, uh, suitable."

"Then why did you marry Richard?" Mary Ellen asked.

"Oh, I thought it might work out. But he moved us to that awful place where I didn't know anyone. There was nothing to do. The only cultural activity there is the one movie house. And Richard was never a real husband to me. He was gone a lot. I think he has a mistress."

"Then why didn't you get a divorce?"

"It's not that easy. I talked about it with my sister and once with my mother. They both told me to keep trying to make the marriage work. Mother said the family would not tolerate the disgrace of a divorce."

"So you got in touch with Hanley and began corresponding in coded letters?" Marcus asked.

"She was desperate," Hanley interjected. "She had to get out. We thought she could just disappear, get an apartment near where I work, and live quietly. I guess we were pretty naïve."

"That's an understatement," Marcus said emphatically.

"And what have you been doing while Hanley is working at the CCC camp?" Mary Ellen asked.

"I've been going to college—graduate work in English literature. I've kept busy."

"And who is paying your bills? This apartment, food, tuition—who is paying for all that?"

"Hanley makes a salary, and my sister sends me money."

"Your sister knows about all this?" Marcus asked irately.

"Yes."

Mary Ellen nodded. "I thought that might be what was going on."

Marcus leaned forward and looked at Amanda. "All right, let's get to the main point here. Did you go with Hanley voluntarily, and have you remained in hiding of your own free will?"

"Yes."

Marcus slapped his hands on his knees. "Then, that's it for now. There has been some deception here—a lot of deception, and there has been wholesale lying and withholding of evidence. You did that, Hanley, when we interviewed you at the CCC camp. And Amanda's sister has withheld evidence and aided and abetted in this deception. And then there is the business of adultery, which is still illegal in this state and carries a pretty heavy penalty. I am going to have to talk with the state's attorney about criminal charges, but for now that's all I am going to do. Neither of you should leave the state, and Amanda—I suggest you get in touch with your parents and husband immediately and try to explain what you have done. I am going to notify the FBI and call off the search. Tomorrow morning, I will release the whole story to the press, so you had better be ready for that."

Marcus stood and looked at Mary Ellen. "Do you have anything to add?"

"Only this—it was wrong to do what you did, Amanda, but I'm glad you weren't kidnapped or murdered."

Amanda began to cry.

"OK," said Marcus, "let's go."

# CHAPTER 16

As soon as they were in the car, Mary Ellen wanted to know what Marcus intended to do about Amanda and Hanley.

"I'm not sure yet. I need to talk with the state's attorney. They sure have caused everyone a lot of trouble, and they have probably broken some laws, but I'm not ready to say how they should be punished. It was a sneaky and juvenile thing to do. They didn't seem to care what problems they caused."

"They are in love."

"Yeah." Marcus laid his hand on hers. "I guess that makes a difference. I'm not sure I would have thought that way two weeks ago."

Mary Ellen smiled and covered his hand with her other one.

After a moment Marcus withdrew his hand, causing Mary Ellen to look at him in surprise.

"What's wrong?" she asked, sensing as she did that Marcus needed to get on more official terms.

"Nothing wrong. I was just thinking about what charges to bring against Amanda and Hanley."

Mary Ellen's mind raced. She had been thinking about Amanda as a victim. Running off with Hanley did not seem like much of a crime.

Almost defensively, she said, "Tell me Marcus, what laws have they broken?"

"Well, I can think of two: obstruction of justice and adultery."

"Adultery! That's a crime?"

"Yep. Has been since back in the 1880's. You haven't heard of it because there hasn't been a prosecution for adultery in Jefferson County for maybe twenty years, but the law is still on the books. You can get jail time for adultery in Illinois."

"So why isn't it prosecuted?"

"I guess it's just a matter of changing attitudes. It sure isn't because there hasn't been any adultery. I expect it's flourishing, as usual."

"So if you were going to prosecute a case of adultery, when would you do it? When you catch someone in the act?"

"That would be a clear cut case, but I'm not about to go busting into motel rooms or people's houses trying to catch some guy in bed with another man's wife."

"Why not?" Mary Ellen chuckled, thinking of what a possible scene might look like. "It sounds like fun."

"Well, it wouldn't be. How would you like to . . . oh, never mind."

"Sheriff, I think you are getting embarrassed."

"Yeah, but let's get serious. In prosecutions for adultery, living together is usually sufficient evidence to establish the case."

"And that's what we have here," Mary Ellen said.

Marcus agreed. "But the law against adultery is antiquated. It goes back to when the lawmakers were trying to force people to live by the Ten Commandments."

Mary Ellen was silent for a while. Then she asked, "Which one of the Commandments is adultery?"

"Darned if I know."

"It's pretty far down the list—about seven I think." she observed.

"And as I said, the law hasn't been enforced. Maybe we ought to forget about it."

Mary Ellen smiled. "Sounds good to me."

"OK. If the state's attorney doesn't bring it up, I won't either."

"Then what about the obstruction of justice charge?" Mary Ellen looked at Marcus to see what his reaction would be.

"That's a little different. What Friedman did was exactly that. He knew we were looking for her when he set her up in that apartment, and he lied to us when we interviewed him. When he did that, he was getting directly in the way of our investigation. If that isn't obstruction of justice, I don't know what is. He did it intentionally, and it led to all kinds of unnecessary problems including the shooting of an FBI agent and almost getting you killed. We can't just overlook what he did. I think the state's attorney will want to charge him. I'm going to recommend it."

"Would there be a trial?"

"I don't know. It would depend on how his lawyer wants to handle it. He could plead Friedman out and get a light sentence, probably probation and some public service. But if it goes to trial and there is a jury, there's no telling what the outcome would be. A good lawyer could work up a certain amount of sympathy for Friedman—you know, a couple in love, a wife caught in a loveless marriage."

Mary Ellen added, "It wouldn't take a whole lot of investigation to find out about Newcombe's affair with Maureen, would it?"

"You may be right, but how would you prove it? We're back to the same question."

"I see what you are saying. All we saw at Tom's Place that night was two people having dinner together. But I would be willing to bet that they have a place they go to—a motel or hotel. That would prove something."

"Do you know of any places like that?" Marcus asked with a grin.

"No!" She answered quickly. "Do You?"

Marcus ducked the question and returned to what might happen in a trial. "The defense might get Hanley off completely," he reasoned. "There would probably be at least a few people on a jury that would not want to send a guy to jail for the kind of thing Friedman did, especially if it's a local jury given the ill feelings around here toward Newcombe. One or two on a jury against a conviction is all you need for an acquittal."

"So if you recommend that Hanley be prosecuted, there is still a good chance he will not have to do any time in jail?"

"Probably not, at least that's the way it looks to me."

"And what about Diedra, Amanda's sister? She knew what they were doing and was even sending them money. Do you think she should be charged?"

"When you interviewed her, did you ask her directly if she knew where her sister was?"

Mary Ellen thought for a minute. "No, it never came up—I never asked. I should have, shouldn't I?"

"Yeah, I suppose so.  But if she never actually lied to you about it, there was no crime."

"What about sending money?"

"Um, I guess we could make a case that sending money was aiding and abetting the crime of adultery, but if we are going to more or less ignore the crime, we ought to ignore someone who aided it. Besides, she might have been sending her sister money without knowing that she was living with Hanley."

"Oh, I think she knew what was going on."

"Well, it's up to you; since you are the one that interviewed her, but I would say forget it."

"She was actually quite cooperative. She helped me in finding Amanda's hidden code. You're right. I will forget it."

Marcus drove in silence for a while. Finally, he turned to Mary Ellen and said simply, "You were great. This case would not have been solved without what you did."

"Thanks. I guess I did do pretty well. Can I have a real detective's badge now? I'm still wearing this old deputy's badge."

"We already ordered it."

Mary Ellen was happy. She *had* done a lot to solve the case, and the outcome wasn't bad. And through all of it, she had come to understand Marcus and in the process had fallen in love with him. He was a reasonable man. No softie, but a man who was able to see the human side of things.  Once he knew all the facts, he would take the actions that were best for everyone involved—at least the innocent ones. Sure, he was a sheriff, but he was a sheriff with a heart—a great big heart that she loved.  No doubt he would enforce the law, and he would see to it that crimes were punished, but he would do it with an even hand and compassion.

He would be a fine husband.

Mary Ellen settled into her seat and smiled as she gazed out the open window of the Chevy. Scattered patches of forest rolled by, green rows of corn sparkled in the mid-day sun, and a red-tailed hawk circled in the blue sky. Southern Illinois might not be ritzy like the Gold Coast in Chicago, but it was a fine place to live. She and Marcus were going to have good lives together here, and if he needed a detective for an interesting case, well . . . she would always be available.

"You know," she said after a long silence, "we thought at one point that this was a case where someone—maybe Richard Newcombe—had tried to commit a perfect murder."

"Yeah," said Marcus. "And . . ."

"And it *was* a perfect murder. Nobody got killed."

LaVergne, TN USA
24 February 2010
173906LV00004B/34/P